COYOTE IN
MANHATTAN

COYOTE IN MANHATTAN

JEAN CRAIGHEAD GEORGE

Illustrated by John Kaufmann

THOMAS Y. CROWELL COMPANY
NEW YORK

By the Author

Coyote in Manhattan
Gull Number 737
Hold Zero!
My Side of the Mountain
Spring Comes to the Ocean
The Summer of the Falcon

Contents

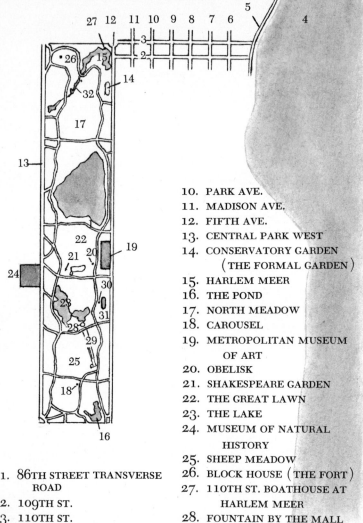

10. PARK AVE.
11. MADISON AVE.
12. FIFTH AVE.
13. CENTRAL PARK WEST
14. CONSERVATORY GARDEN
    (THE FORMAL GARDEN)
15. HARLEM MEER
16. THE POND
17. NORTH MEADOW
18. CAROUSEL
19. METROPOLITAN MUSEUM
    OF ART
20. OBELISK
21. SHAKESPEARE GARDEN
22. THE GREAT LAWN
23. THE LAKE
24. MUSEUM OF NATURAL
    HISTORY
25. SHEEP MEADOW
26. BLOCK HOUSE (THE FORT)
27. 110TH ST. BOATHOUSE AT
    HARLEM MEER
28. FOUNTAIN BY THE MALL
29. THE MALL
30. HANS CHRISTIAN ANDERSON
    STATUE
31. CONSERVATORY POND
    (MODEL BOATING)
32. THE LOCH

1. 86TH STREET TRANSVERSE
   ROAD
2. 109TH ST.
3. 110TH ST.
4. EAST RIVER
5. EAST RIVER DRIVE
6. 1ST AVE.
7. 2ND AVE.
8. 3RD AVE.
9. LEXINGTON AVE.

TAKO'S CENTRAL PARK
AND NEARBY STREETS

109th Street

She was on the hot sidewalk in front of number 35 on East 109th Street, New York City. Harlem murmured behind her. Around the corner to the left Park Avenue gleamed in the sun, and to her right Central Park rustled.

The afternoon air was glassy with reflected heat. It was August, August 24, to be exact. Tenny Harkness, high school freshman-to-be, was playing a game. It was called Go Meet Daddy. She didn't want to play it. It always led to an argument and tears. But she would, because it was expected of her.

She glanced up at her converted-brownstone

apartment house. It was now painted gray, and a frieze of hand-scrawled drawings, names, and battle cries defaced the once handsome archway. She just glanced, not reading "Zop the Street Family" or "Alvie fight Fredrico." She was concentrating on the game.

It always began as it had today. First her mother screamed from the closet-kitchen: "Tenny, git down there and meet that freighter. Your dad'll be in a boil if no one's there!" Following this came the pause and then the line, "After all he *is* your father."

This initiated the next part of the game. Tenny would open her bureau drawer, take out a clean shirt, and put it on. She would go to the sink and wash her face. As she rinsed the soap away she would look long into the mirror. She thought the walnut color of her skin was quite beautiful. It set off her large black eyes with their curled lashes, and it glowed dark under her cheek bones and around her firm chin. Then she would analyze her flared nostrils and full lips and wonder if her father was going to call her "kindergarten face" today, and why he did. Alone at the mirror she thought she was growing into a pretty woman.

This thought was always shattered as she walked down the three dark flights of steps to the front door and anticipated meeting her father. She knew he would tell her she was too fat or that her hairdo was ridiculous. By the time she reached the street she would have reanalyzed herself. She *was* too heavy and her face *was* childlike. In this state of mind the criticism was easier to bear. After that came the next part of the game. She would whisper, "Maybe it'll be different this time."

"Maybe it'll be different this time," she said and turned doggedly toward Madison Avenue, a trench of trucks and cars that cut through a headstream of buildings.

The game usually went pleasantly until she got to the freighter, met her father, was hurt by his words, and walked home behind him, head down, wishing she could take criticism.

Today, however, the game changed. It happened just before she reached the railroad tracks that arched over the street and carried the commuter trains downtown.

She saw José Amando. According to the game she wasn't supposed to see anyone she knew on her way. The sixteen-year-old Puerto Rican was under his green car that he had coaxed into action from parts and pieces he had gathered at Joe's Auto Repair down by the East River. José was the most important young man in the "Street Family," the high

3

school group from 109th Street. He called the meetings, thought of places to go and things to do, and saw to it that they avoided trouble. The Family looked to José for decisions, and although the other four male members argued with him, they eventually followed his leadership. He was pleasant about insisting.

Tenny's summer hope, now that she was entering the senior high school across town, was that the Street Family would accept her. They had admitted her best friends—Elaine Bedford, red-headed, freckled, and Australian, and Maria La Gloria, golden-skinned, plump, and Italian—because, it was said, they could both sing. The Street Family spent hours making up songs and singing. They sang about life on 109th Street—about stick-ball games, a sand company's sand where no one could play, the police, taxis, and characters like Mrs. La Gloria, who ran the grocery store, whom they called "our street mayor," and Joe "the freedom man," who repaired old automobiles. Since much of their time was spent airing conflicts with parents, uncles, brothers and sisters, they improvised songs about home life, too.

Tenny sang, but ever since her father had said her voice sounded like a river of tears, she sang only where no one could hear her. When she was up on the roof hanging clothes, if the traffic was heavy and the boats whistling, she would perform for the chimney and the pigeons.

As she recognized José's sandaled feet under the car she was reminded of the last time she had played the game. On the way home he had caught up with her. He had been so pleasant. He had proudly asked her about the honors she had received in mathematics that day. She had been so happy to talk about the achievement her father had called "a waste of time for a girl." She had lifted her head, forgotten about the argument with her father, and smiled all the way down the block—an inside smile.

At home, however, her father had shut the door, then grabbed her by her shoulders. "I don't want to see you messin' around with none of those trashy boys," he had shouted. She gasped, "But that was José!" Then she realized that her father was away too much to know what kind of a boy José was. She was about to tell him when he growled between his teeth, "Whatdaya think he wants? A friend?" Tenny had felt sick. She had run to the bathroom, the only room with a door that locked, and had sat there for an hour holding her ears.

5

This was always the end of the game—holding her head and forgetting her father's words. She was able to get rid of the misery by imagining herself performing a wonderful and gentle deed that would turn the eyes of the world admiringly upon her. Even her father would be pleased. The last time she had led a group of children out of a burning building.

Tenny was shaken out of her memories as she passed under the railroad bridge and a train rumbled overhead. The last trip to the boat roared out of her mind. She was about to go on with the present game, repeating for the next two blocks "Maybe it'll be different, maybe it'll be different," when the game changed again. She met Elaine Bedford.

Elaine was stepping out of her red-brick apartment house between Lexington and Third avenues. She and Tenny had been in the same class since third grade and Tenny had often spent the night with the Bedfords when she was younger. Mr. and Mrs. Bedford encouraged her visits, for she patiently taught Elaine math while they played. The Bedfords had called her "the tutor" and declared that Elaine passed the subject only because her friend was a living computer.

Tenny stopped and waited for Elaine, noticing her wet curls. She had probably been swimming at the 111th Street pool. As Tenny studied her silky walk she realized she had not seen Elaine for a long time.

"How's life?" Tenny called.

"Fine," Elaine said curtly. They walked in silence to the end of the block before Tenny had the courage to speak her mind. "The Street Family, Elaine?" she whispered. "Do you think they'll let me in?"

"No!" Elaine blurted. She was a blunt-spoken girl who was never able to dissemble. Now, because Tenny was so still, she jabbered on. "They voted on you. They discuss everyone first. Everyone feels you're kinda way out—kinda 'removed.' They like you. I mean, they think you're bright and all; but, well, you're a little too do-goody for us."

"Did *you* vote for me?" Tenny's voice was low with dread but she had to know.

"Well, ah—no!" Elaine said. "You know how it is. You understand."

Tenny stepped fast now. She crossed the avenue on a red light, leaving Elaine on the curb, and ran the distance to the end of 109th Street. She turned north, forgetting all about the game until she was on the walkway over the East River Drive. It took great will to erase Elaine from her mind, but she did it for a moment and began repeating, "Maybe it'll be different this time."

She walked down the ramp to the narrow row of benches that faced the river. The old men who watched the ships were not there. It was too hot for them to sit in the sun, so they were somewhere in the shadows of the buildings now. At the great brick warehouse and shipping dock of the Washburn Wire Company she went on with the rules.

"If he'll try, I'll try," she said, concentrating on her father. But the words didn't come out right. Elaine's words came back like a physical assault. Tenny's bones burned and a deep sob choked her.

She opened the door to the warehouse and dock. The air smelled of clean steel and burned oil. She concentrated very hard, walked through one of the huge rolls of wire, ran out into the sun and across gray boards to the freighter. Again the game had changed. Her father was not on the deck where he always was, tying the lines to secure the ship to the dock.

Tenny walked up the gangplank. No one was around. Maybe it'll be different this time, she thought; but it all looked the same. The metal decks were hot and clean, the big engines at the rear of the ship were throbbing to a soft stop, and the superstructure shone white and salty at the front. She started toward the stern. Perhaps her father was still down in the engine room.

Then everything did change. She saw a wooden cage in the shadow of the pilot house. Flies hovered over it; something alive was in it. She ran to the wire-fronted crate. A doglike animal was curled in the corner. She was not sure what he was. He was almost the size and color of a small shep-

9

herd dog, and she thought at first he must be a puppy. Then he lifted his head and she saw his eyes. They were wild as the forest, and disconcertingly yellow. Tenny bit her thumb nail in wonderment. A voice came from the pilot house.

"Leon," a man said, "you'd better git that durn coyote off this ship before the Health Inspector comes aboard."

"Goawann," Tenny heard her father answer. "I know all the inspectors on this river. I'll git him off when I'm ready."

Tenny did not move to meet her father. She bent down to the coyote. He pressed his ears back and shifted his eyes suspiciously. Then he sniffed and his expression seemed to soften. He moved toward her.

The man's voice came again. "Whatya gonna do with him, Leon? Give him to your kid?" Tenny's mouth opened in surprise and hope. Maybe he *is* trying, she thought. A coyote, he's bringing me a coyote. She kneeled down beside the grayish-gold animal.

"I ain't givin' Tako to no kid," said her father. "He's worth a hundred bucks. A friend of mine who's got a pet store wants him. I can make a hundred bucks go a long way."

Tenny stopped hoping. She put her hands on the cage. "Tako," she whispered.

This is the last move of the game, she thought— the gentle deed. But it's real this time. I can really do something, not dream it. "Tako," she whispered again. "I'm gonna let you go."

Tako

The coyote stood up. A girl was speaking to him. He instantly knew her sex. It was one of the first things he recognized in any animal. Next he judged movements. Hers were gentle but anxious. He checked the ship's deck quickly. A flag twisted in the wind. A bell clanged. The ship moved up and down with the breathing of the tidal river. There seemed to be nothing to fear there. The coyote glanced beyond the ship. A butte of buildings rose in blocks and squares. The sun snapped off glass windows making a thousand smaller suns, and a blue mist sifted upward like the haze of a hot desert dawn. Tako had slept so hard the last seven hours that he had not known when the ship stopped moving. Although he had been in port two hours, he had not seen New York City until this moment. He lifted his head and smelled it. No scents of sagebrush or birds came to him, just the irritating odor of burned gases and oil. He tuned his ears to the city. His hearing was so acute it added images to his other senses. The sounds were hard, unlike the warm pounding of cattle hoofs or the thump of jack rabbit feet on the desert clay. There were ringings and clangings, low metallic roars and a high thin hum. Tako knew all he needed to know about New York City. It was riddled with people. He turned his gaze on the girl.

As her fingers played over the latch of his cage he felt in her an attitude new for a human being —warmth. He reacted to this. He responded to attitudes, smells, postures, bodily expressions. He sensed the girl was survival. So, drawing on his entire five months of experiences, he rallied to this one event.

Tako had been born in April in a den on the hot dry plains beyond Corpus Christi, Texas. The den had been dug into an open hillside by his mother. It had a clear view of the eroded valley and the dry river bed below it. The coyote had been born at twilight and his mother had licked him for almost an hour, turning him gently with her nose as he crept toward her belly and her milk-filled mammae. The two of them had been very quiet. Wild birth is a silent and odorless thing to prevent detection.

The next kit was born dead. Tako knew nothing of this, nor of the careful eradication of the lifeless animal by his mother. He was affected by it, however. The devotion she would have given the second kit was turned upon him. She licked him, played with him, and cared for him so affectionately that he had a strong sense of independence and confidence before the sun ever rose. He slept through the arrival of the next two kits, females, and smaller than he. Many hours later, he felt their warm bodies snuggling against his, and this, too, was pleasant.

The next few weeks were the same: food, affection, and clambering den mates. Then vision came to Tako and with it the presence of another individual—his father. The big male coyote came to the den entrance bringing food to Tako's mother. At these times he nudged her, then lay down at the den to guard the family.

As the days passed and Tako gained strength, he was able to wobble toward this grizzled-buff parent. He found his father aloof but interested. He watched him and his sisters as they ventured closer and closer to the den entrance. One day Tako rushed out into the sun. His father attacked him with such anger that he was cowed and lay low. Now he was aware of two new emotions—his father's wrath and his own fear. The old male stood by a rock and snarled softly as a rattlesnake slid past the den.

Incident by incident the young coyote learned to use his senses. His father watched hawks in the sky. Tako followed his gaze and watched them too. His father opened his nostrils to judge scents and Tako learned to use his nose. By observing his father he also learned to listen for the crackle of grasshoppers or the distant footsteps of people. He recognized the sound of a dog "ambling" as compared to its "hunting" with men.

By the time he was weaned in June and other coyote families came out of their dens on the dry river bench, he had learned to recognize his own kind. Through smelling, watching, and listening he became aware of individual coyotes. He learned the smell of a pup his own age and sex from urine

on the urine-posts. At these spots he also learned the odor of dominant males of the region.

The messages in the urine kept the coyote population informed in other ways. Fear tainted the urine and alerted the reader to danger, while contentment smelled sweet and brought relaxation. From the coyote feces he learned what food the other animal had caught and he set out to hunt the same. During these weeks he also became familiar with the physical poses of animal emotion—aggression, play, affection; each was expressed in a stance, and often a scent.

Tako's family stayed together even after the pups were weaned. They hunted by night and day in an intelligent, coyote manner. Trotting to the crest of the hill they took off for the live oak woods according to the wind. They traveled into it. It blew their scent behind so that the prey ahead would not be warned of their approach. Tako's family went far; they never took a rodent or bird near the den, for instinctively they knew how to "farm." The animal crop near at hand was cultivated for times of stress, then reaped in such a way that there would always be more. They also had other canny methods. In the plains the whole family would often play dead in order to surprise a road runner or a sage grouse. They chased mice to each other to catch and finally, with remarkable animal insight, they would return home by a circuitous route so as to lose their enemies and confuse their prey.

In July the pups learned to wail. Sitting on a mound in the open they yipped and called with their parents. Other coyote families answered them until dawn and dusk quivered with the eerie orchestra of the coyotes.

Around the first of August Tako's curiosity and independence changed the course of his life. His parents were off hunting when two men drove up in a jeep. Tako came out of the den to watch and smell. They were sweaty and hot, but no scent or pose indicated that they were aggressive. They placed a rectangular box on the ground and got back into the jeep. One of the men was Leon Harkness, Tenny's father and boatswain on the Washburn Wire Company freighter.

Tako came forward curiously. As he studied the box the wind brought him the scent of fresh meat. He moved gingerly toward a live trap. For a moment he was not sure whether to investigate or run. His father was not there to warn or encourage him, so the young coyote followed his own impulse—investigate. He slipped closer. The long metal box, four feet by two by two, was differently bright, intriguing—and one end was open. Inside lay the meat. Tako sniffed for the men. He smelled only the steel and oil of the jeep.

Tako dove into the box. The weight of his paws tripped a hook. The steel door slammed. Tako was a captive. He rushed, he bit, powered by the fear and anger that had given him energy to get out of other dangerous predicaments. He was confused by its failure now.

Then the men appeared. They ran toward him shouting. They lifted him excitedly and carried him to the jeep. He was driven to a dock in Corpus

Christi and then he was transferred to the ship.

The next morning Leon came to him. Tako snarled and pulled into a compact ball, ears back, fangs bared.

"You look like a Chinese kite I once had." The man laughed. "Had broom weeds on it, and a mean face. Tako—that's what the Chinese called that kite. Tako. That's what I'll call you." Leon lifted the trap and dumped Tako into a big wooden cage with a wire front and a steel-rimmed door. The man offered him food. Tako snatched it. Leon talked to him. Then he went away.

For the next week while the ship sat in port, Leon spent long hours with Tako; and the coyote called upon all his wisdom, canniness, and instinct to understand this human animal who had taken his father's role and was bringing him food. He never trusted him; in fact, he feared him. Yet Leon fed him and hunted for him. Tako transferred his respect for his father to the brown cloth-covered man. He was too young to do anything else. He still needed a father, even a fear-inspiring one.

During the day, Leon would sit beside him and scratch his head. It felt good. In this peace Tako listened to his voice. He responded to its barks and soothings, its laughter and fear. The words meant nothing, but the attitudes were clear. As he sensed and reacted he learned. However, he never became tame. That spark of animal independence that Tako's mother had given him the first night of his birth was too strong to be trampled. He learned to adjust to Leon, but he never loved him. He constantly watched for a chance to escape, for not only was the cage confining, but the noises and stenches of the boat were painful to his ears and nose.

On a hot afternoon, the tanker sailed out of Corpus Christi. For several hours the movement bothered Tako, then he adjusted to it.

During the next three days he met other men. They stood over his cage and talked to him. Gradually he learned to relax in their presence. One day Leon opened the door and let him out. Tako knew enough about Leon's anger and dominance not to run. Instead he followed him much as he had followed his parents, as all young must follow. This evoked both laughter and some sort of satisfaction not only from Leon but from the other men as well, and Tako stored this reaction in his animal brain.

One evening the ship docked in New Orleans. While Tako was sleeping the men went ashore. He was awakened at midnight when Leon sat down by his cage and sang to him. Tako sensed play in his

wails and trills, and also something he didn't understand—the loss of physical control caused by alcohol. A man called, and Leon lumbered away. An hour later Tako felt the movement of the sea.

The trip up the coast began. Each morning Tako was permitted to follow Leon. Once he dove toward the edge of the ship to escape. Leon hurled a monkey wrench at him and snarled, "Git back here, Tako!" The coyote lunged on, saw the water below the ship, and slunk back to Leon's heels.

Daily walks grew into excursions of freedom until the ship was two days out of New York, then Tako was not released any more. By now the cage was foul and dirty, despite the fact that, in his clean coyote manner, he had kept his body wastes in one corner. But this area was too small for a wide-ranging animal. The ship's rats came to the cage at night for the refuse and leftover food. They dropped eggs that hatched into larvae and fleas. He became flea-ridden.

One night Tako smelled "green." He paced his cage wildly for this was the aroma of land—his environment.

On the morning of August 24, tired from the strain of confinement, Tako retreated into sleep. He curled into a tight ball, pulled his bushy tail over his nose, and did not even hear the ship blasts and stirs as the human beings came home.

Then the girl sat down by the cage.

She was quite different from Leon. Her attitude was gentle and motherly. He trusted this far more than Leon's brutal dominance. He stepped forward when he heard the final click of the latch and saw the door of his cage swing open. The girl whispered, "Yes, this time it *is* different." The words meant nothing to him, but her attitude did. He followed her, knowing intuitively that she meant survival. He trusted her as he had trusted his parents. He forgot the fear-inspiring Leon.

Tenny led him quickly to the edge of the ship and down the gangplank to the shipping dock of the Washburn Wire Company, East 118th Street, New York City.

He concentrated on the girl. She ran to the shipping room. He followed. She walked through corridors of wire. Alert to men in a far corner, Tenny walked faster. Tako did, too. His shoulder blades rippled as his legs carried him like an eagle's shadow to the door.

Tenny opened it, and suddenly Tako was in the sunlight on hot white cement at the edge of the quaking city. He moved closer to the girl, threw the jagged wall of buildings a calculating glance, perceived that the city bore no smell of the earth, but that a pigeon winged overhead. Where a bird could live so could he.

The girl tensed, looked back at the wire company in fear, and darted off. Tako turned, too, and looked back for Leon. He could taste her feelings. She was as obvious as his testy, cautious mother.

Tenny led him past the benches. Parallel shadows lay under them, and for an instant Tako thought of running into their shade. Judgment told him, however, that they were not enough to hide him, and so he urged himself on.

The girl slowed down to a walk as she glanced nervously at an old woman on a bench. Tako sensed her worry and when Tenny hesitated, Tako hesitated. All strange animals were something to size up before acting, but particularly people. Fear of men was deep in the coyote, even in Tako, despite his life among them. Furthermore, he was on unfamiliar ground, and this too made him cautious. Tenny whistled. He trotted beside her. They passed the woman unnoticed. The coyote noted this success, for, in the manner of all animal life, he learned from success and failure. What he did not know was the reason for his success. He could not know that he had behaved like a dog and this together with his doglike appearance had kept the woman from becoming concerned. Although Tako sensed some tension between Tenny and the other people, he could not know that he was being "sneaked" into New York City. He just stayed at her heels for that was successful.

Suddenly a gull above the river recognized him. The bird screamed the "enemy" cry and wheeled over Tako's head. Two more gulls joined the first. Tako nervously glanced back at the woman, testing whether she understood the alarm and would attack. She did not move. No aggression tightened her muscles. He glanced up at the birds and jogged on behind the girl. He relaxed. The woman, he sensed, did not understand what the gulls had said.

He passed dusty sycamore trees that bristled with the odors of pigeons and starlings. Their trunks and roots vibrated with urine messages from the dogs of the city. These, like coyote urine, informed the domestic canines of the moods and doings of the dog community. Tako read them hastily until he came upon one that announced pups. He glanced at Tenny to see if she was interested. Pups were always a cause for reaction. She did not respond. He added to his learning. She did not smell messages.

He followed Tenny to the 116th Street ramp. The foot bridge over the highway reeked of people, and Tako tightened his stride. As he started over the hazy river of mechanical objects, he saw four men. They were leaning on their elbows gazing into the flow of cars. Walking closer to Tenny as he approached them, he was relieved that they did not turn from their car gazing.

Then Tenny turned and spoke to him. "Come on, Tako," she said. "Here, Tako." She whistled. The men continued to stare into the roaring flume of cars.

He came to another ramp. It led down into a dry park where trees and grass grew. The odor of people dominated the air. As Tako started down, fear seized him. He crouched to flee, but was blocked by people and, beyond them, a crisscross of what he recognized as cage wire. He concentrated on Tenny again and kept close to her feet. They moved with ease, passing women and children, men and clusters of boys. None reacted to his presence.

Tenny turned a corner and faced the roll and drum of the city. She started down a long sidewalk, walled with a pool bathhouse on the right and tennis courts on the left. Benches lined the walk and each was filled with seated New Yorkers. Tako sensed the danger of passing through so many people but he had no choice. He had to follow like a duckling behind its mother.

Not a single person got up to fight his entrance into the city. This was difficult for Tako to understand. He was a stranger invading new territory—a trespasser. In the wild, trespassing stirred violent reactions—conflict and aggression—so Tako moved with caution, listening, smelling, watching.

The wind was blowing off the river toward the city, carrying his scent to the one animal who could smell a stranger. A dog caught his odor and, in a volley of barks, announced Tako's presence. The coyote looked for a route of escape and felt for a wind that would carry off his scent. Spotting a hidden trail between the benches and the pool wall, he slipped to the right and vanished onto a checkerboard of sunlight and shadows, and into an envelope of people smells. He trotted past the dog that jumped in confusion at the end of a leash, sniffing the air, pulling his master in an effort to find the lost wind that had brought Tako to him. He leaped and dug the sidewalk with his claws.

Tenny kept moving. She came to the end of the walk and waited. Tako trotted to the last bench, stepped into the off-river wind, and slipped quietly to her side. He glanced back at the excited dog.

The retriever barked once more, told the people a stranger was in their midst, and was silenced.

As Tako listened he became aware of a man staring at him. He sat down as he had done when Leon stared at him. A scrutinizing glance made him afraid, for predators like Tako only stared when stalking. Tako sat still before the man's gaze; in hunting jack rabbits he had learned the sitting ones were hard to see. He needed to be as inconspicuous as possible before the staring predator.

"That's a weird dog," the man said to Tenny.

"He's a japotta," she invented quickly. He mumbled something, went on, and Tenny leaned down to Tako. She spoke. Her words were meaningless, but the gentleness he had sensed when they met sang through the sounds she made. "Stay close to me, Tako. I will get you to Central Park." She became animated. "Then you can hide in the trees and bushes. You can run and play with the pigeons and sparrows." Patting his head, she made a slight gesture toward the street. Tako stood up, not because of what she had said but because she had reacted to a light. She kept her eyes on it. It flashed. So sensitive was the coyote to gestures that he could anticipate her movements. He walked before she did.

They quietly crossed the street and turned south.

Tako

Tenny led him past a deserted school, around a fenced playground, and into dusty winds. She stopped at 109th Street and spoke to him once more. "This is my street," she said, "and the park is at the end of it. Good luck, pretty Tako." She smoothed her blue skirt and stepped forward.

The coyote twitched his ears and listened, but his eyes and his nose were on other matters. Both sides of the street were burrowed with steps that led into dark cellars. The air that rose from the nearest one was dank with the odor of rats. He relaxed. There was food for him in the canyons of the men.

Tenny hurried. Tako followed, jogging from cellar to cellar to investigate the scents. All at once a fresh rat smell rose off the sidewalk in front of him. He traced it to the curb and lost it in an oily slick of water that pooled in the gutter. Paper floated in it, and hundreds of odorous bird steps at its edges indicated that the city flourished with pigeons and sparrows as well as rats.

Intensely aware that he was a stranger and open to attack, Tako felt the need for a den pressing him toward cellars and trash cans. He investigated as many as possible while still keeping pace with Tenny. In the debris along the wall of the sand-

trucking company, he aroused a flea. It catapulted
to his nose, and Tako snapped at the first wild crea-
ture in New York to welcome him to the city. The
insect burrowed through his buff-colored fur, found
a spot near his ear, and bit. Tako sat down and
scratched vigorously, then glanced up to see Tenny
hurrying ahead, tense and alarmed. He responded
to her fears by searching for a hideout.

He swept into the dark shadows along the side of
a building. When he had traveled the length of it
he was in the open, headed for Joe's Auto Repair. It
was a yard of junked cars. He glided under one,
crouched, and studied Tenny. She was nervous.
Her leg muscles were tight. Her hands opened
and closed. A man approached her. She faced him
testily, and the conversation that ensued was to
change Tako's destiny in the city.

The Meeting

The man was a lean Negro, neatly dressed and full of purpose. When he saw Tenny he smiled. "Hi," he said with a lilt of surprise. "I'm just on my way to your father's ship."

"Aw," Tenny blundered. "Aw—uh, hello, Mr. Evans." Her hands dived into her skirt pockets. She glanced behind her, did not see Tako, and turned back to face the man. "Are *you* inspecting his ship today?" she asked with forced brightness.

"Sure am," he answered. "Just routine. Just routine. They put in at New Orleans this trip. The town's been known to have rats with plague-infested fleas and so we check ships that touch there."

"Plague-infested fleas?"

"Yes, indeed."

"Sounds like the thirteenth century."

"Not at all. The threat is always around, although we've learned to pretty much control it." He seemed to want to talk, but Tenny wanted to go.

"We check every ship that's been to a foreign port and even some American ports where there've been outbreaks. That's my main job as a U. S. Health Inspector, you know, checking for diseases that might come into the city."

"Well, I sorta knew that," Tenny said as she wondered what to do about Tako, who had now disappeared.

"Routine, just routine," Cardy Evans went on persistently. "New York's never had an outbreak, but we don't dare not check. The plague's a horror." Tenny tried to leave. Mr. Evans spoke louder. "It's transmitted by fleas that bite infected rats. They bite other animals and they bite people, and the people're dead in five days." She tried once more to go on but this time he stopped her with a hand on her shoulder.

"Tenny," he said, "I saw you coming up the block with a strange-looking dog at your heels. Where is he?"

"Dog?" Tenny began to feel the stirrings of panic. Why wouldn't he let her go? "What dog?" she asked.

"Well, funny thing, I don't think it was a dog." Mr. Evans glanced down the sidewalk. "I was stationed in the New Mexico desert during the war, and got to know coyotes. I don't think I'd miss that low-slung bushy tail and sleek saunter. I think I saw a coyote."

The Meeting

Tenny felt a hot rush of fear tingling in her neck. Her oval eyes rounded. "Oh, that dog?" she blurted. "I don't know, he was just ambling along with me . . . I guess he went home."

Mr. Evans tweaked her cheek. "Come on." He smiled. "I've known you and your daddy too long . . . coming to meet him when the ship's in and all. You can talk to me. Besides, it's really dangerous to have wild animals in the city. They bring in parasites and disease . . . the plague, Tenny. They're finding it in chipmunks and other little animals in the national parks. Will you tell me something about the dog?"

"A dog?" Tenny whispered. "I don't know what you're talking about."

"Rumor, just rumor," he said.

"What kind of rumor, Mr. Evans?"

"Oh, a phone call from a New Orleans' health inspector. He picked up a rumor that a man in a bar by the wharves had a coyote and was taking it to New York City to sell. It happened to be your daddy's ship the man was on . . . and so I'm off to work."

"Well." Tenny was frightened. Her kind deed was becoming a menace. She turned all the way around. "I don't see anything, do you?"

"No." Mr. Evans patted her shoulder. "Just odd,

that when I'm walking down to check the rumor of a coyote on a ship, I think I see one."

Tenny smiled at him. "You always did live your work, Mr. Evans." The inspector laughed. He stroked his square chin and close-cut hair.

"You're probably right," he said. "See you later, Tenny."

There was something in his voice that made Tenny feel that he *would* see her later. She hurried across the street not looking for Tako for fear Cardy Evans was watching. She had to think. At First Avenue she glanced around. Mr. Evans was out of sight. She waited, then started back, feeling as she hurried along that maybe she had missed her chance to perform the real heroic deed, not just daydream it. She could save the city from the threat of plague. The idea made her dizzy with pleasure. Then the nausea of conflict sickened her. She couldn't do it. She was too frightened—too afraid of her father's wrath, too afraid of being punished by the authorities for the harm she had already done—and too proud to admit she had done wrong. It *was* a beautiful deed she had done. The animal was free.

I'm getting all mixed up, she thought, and broke into a run. She came to the sand-trucking company building where she had last seen Tako. He was nowhere to be found. She looked in a cellar, crossed the street, and searched behind boxes and cans. Then she stared at Joe's Auto Repair, the wheels, engines, and dented bodies. She hurried over to it, bent down, and looked under the cars. Finally she stood still in puzzlement.

He's gone, she thought, and that's that. He will be clean and neat and beautiful, and . . . he's free . . . and that's beautiful to think about.

She said hello to Joe who asked if she had lost anything; then she turned west and started slowly home. For the next three blocks she glanced in open cellar wells and down narrow alleys between buildings. Finally she skipped, wishing to put a greater distance between herself, Mr. Evans, the ship, and the coyote. The game *had* to end in a beautiful deed. She would will it to be. The Street Family would recognize its beauty, she thought, and immediately take her in. Tenny ran.

As she came out under the railroad bridge she looked desperately for José. His feet no longer protruded from under the car. She wanted to tell him about Tako and hear his approval, but he wasn't there. Then over the swish of passing cabs and trucks she heard the sound of a musical note and a tapping. It came from the alley beside José's apartment house, another converted brownstone like her own. She crossed the street and wound through dark, hot shadows to the junk-filled court behind the four-story building. José was sitting on a wooden crate in front of the top ten inches of an oil drum, hammering, then listening to the ringing sound. He put his ear down, closed his eyes, and struck a bulge with a leather-tipped drumstick. The sound did not please him. He hammered the metal, making the bulge higher. He lowered his head and

struck again. He rang out a B note, listened, then hit the A note he was working on. The sounds were like chimes. He struck several notes quickly. The court walls echoed with wistful, tinsely notes. Tenny stood still wondering how to begin.

"José," she finally blurted, "I don't want to bother you. Just wanted to tell you that Daddy said he could get some empty oil drums if you ever need them." Now why did I say that? she thought. That's not what I wanted to say at all.

José turned. He pushed his long black hair out of his eyes and said, "Say that again, *petita*."

"If you need any barrels to make steel drums," she repeated, "Dad can get them." Tenny willed him to say no. Leon, she knew, would thunder curses before he gave anything to José.

"I sure *would!*" he answered. José stood up and his long legs bent back gracefully at the knees. "I sure would. I need about four more for a combo." He walked toward her. "Gee, Tenny, that would be great!" He smiled and his smooth lower lip curled slightly off-center, making him engagingly imperfect.

Tenny told him she would let him know when and where, then she turned to leave. José sat down again. He played. The note rang around the court.

It wasn't quite right. He hammered again. Tenny reeled and closed her eyes. Getting the drums, she thought, will be the gentle deed. Letting the coyote go had turned into a nightmare.

She walked down the alley phrasing a conversation with her father. This took such concentration that the whole mixed-up day vanished—Elaine, the Street Family, the coyote, Mr. Evans. Between the narrow alley walls Tenny went off into the world she had to make—a livable world where her father was kind and Elaine was generous, where the coyote was free and Mr. Evans was pleased that he was. As she put one foot on the steps of number 35, she glanced down the long street, quivering with heat waves and congestion. She closed her eyes and the city disappeared. Only the vision of the yellow-eyed coyote remained. He was swinging freely, defying her father, the U. S. Public Health officer—everyone. She chuckled. Laughter tinkled through her chest.

Tenny tucked in her shirt, touched her dark cheeks, and felt pretty again.

Central Park

Tako awoke six hours later between the engine and the fender of a wheelless car into which he had crawled to escape Mr. Evans. It was dark. The hot city was cooling off, cement sidewalks snapped, metal doors and fenders bonged as they contracted in the night air.

Tako lay with his chin on his paws sorting out the sounds of the city. Sparrows chirped behind him as they fought for roosting spots in the cracked wall. Horns tooted far away, a voice called a child in off the streets, and dishes clanged in a restaurant around the corner. Then he took scent. The men who had worked in the repair shop were gone, only their sweat odors remained to remind Tako he had slept among people.

His nostrils flared to gain more information, but he could smell nothing beyond the oily engines and vanished men. He got up and slipped to the ground. A sound made him focus his eyes across the street to where a city garbage truck raced its engine in a garage. Then it backed out and he saw it more clearly. Bulky and large, it began its nightly rounds of the city. As it rolled, Tako heard the scratch of feet on the cars around him. Rats were coming out of their nests. They slid toward the garbage truck, and, anticipating its route, preceded it around the corner. Tako followed the rats. The garbage truck stopped and men jumped from it. They raced to the curb, picked up big cans, opened them, and threw their contents into the rear of the truck. Debris fell. The men climbed into the cab, the engine hummed, and the truck moved down the street.

When it was gone, a ring of rats remained. Tako slid toward them. They were so intent upon each other and the smell of food that they did not sense the coyote. An intelligent sniff told Tako not much food had fallen. Nevertheless, as if at a given signal, the rats moved in upon the gleanings. Their whiskers quivered, their tails stretched straight up in an expression of rat anxiety, for they feared each other more than anything in the city.

Two rats met at a meat wrapper. One snatched it, the other turned upon him. The first dove at his neck. The challenger squealed. Then Tako saw a third rat watching the fight. He was waiting. When the wrapper sailed off in the vigor of the battle he snatched it and darted toward the buildings. Tako leaped upon him. The rat screamed a piercing, fear-

filled cry. The other rats, hearing death, abandoned the street, running hysterically in all directions. There was a wave of movement, then they were gone; down sewers, into holes in the old buildings, back to the junk yard.

Tako took his food to the car lot and devoured it. He was about to go to sleep when a wind changed his mind. He stepped onto the sidewalk and lifted his nose. The wind blew from the west, and was "green" with the scent of trees. To Tako this meant earth and cover. He dashed across the avenue. On the other side he ran onto Tenny's old scent. He tracked along it, for the gentle girl and the smell of trees were in the same direction.

He crossed Second Avenue without incident. The traffic had quieted down for the long hot evening and he crossed unnoticed, his shoulders driving his fur from side to side, his senses tuned sharply to the canyon of the people. The sun had gone down, but a rising glow of light was coming from buildings, cars, and streets. These lights cast dark shadows that Tako noted. He could hide in them.

He did not miss the sounds of cooing pigeons on the sides of the buildings, although a surveying glance told him they were too high for him now, on

45

the window sills and door frames. He nevertheless made a mental image of steps, trash cans, and other aids to height.

Between Second and Third avenues he was forced off Tenny's scent. Men and their dogs were appearing, and again he felt his role as the vulnerable trespasser. He darted under a car parked at the curb, and slid on his belly to the next. He couldn't travel fast here, but he could take stock of the sidewalk and anticipate events by half a block.

Presently he saw a setter approaching, slid behind a wheel, and waited, amusing himself with a candy wrapper that was scratching along in the breeze. He slapped his paw on it, smelled its sweetness, and licked the sugar. It pleased him. The dog passed, his collar jangling, and Tako crept out onto the sidewalk. He heard the wind in the trees and sprinted swiftly on. He crossed Third Avenue and through the distant arch of the railroad bridge saw sycamores and alders bending in the wind. He dropped low and broke into a coyote glide.

At Lexington Avenue, swinging his eyes from right to left, he became aware of new movements. They were high up in the windows above the streets. Here the shadows of people moved in lazy dances as they settled down for the night. Tako already knew that men slept at night and were up by day like the squirrels and birds, and that, like these animals, they too were blind at night. But the city was confusing to him. Within the buildings, small rooms of light enabled the people to see and move with ease. Most of these blocks of light were too high to examine, however, and so, when the doorway of Mrs. La Gloria's *groceria* shone before him, he approached it with curiosity. He sniffed the shaft of light that whitened the pavement, then peered inside the store. Odors of food and people mingled. Hot air swirled about and human voices crackled.

Suddenly the screen door opened and a large yellow tomcat, Mrs. La Gloria's notorious Rancid, stuck his head into the night. His ears and nose were scarred and nicked from cat battles. His neck and shoulders were thick and masculine. He was absolutely confident as he peered across his domain. Tako stepped back, and as he did, Rancid turned his head and stared into Tako's eyes. All the signals of animal aggression went off in both animals and they clamped together like magnets.

Rancid had the advantage. He had razor claws. They ripped down Tako's nose and dug in. Tako was heavier, however. He rolled the cat, dislodged the needles, and snarled down upon his back. Rancid turned and fled. Tako shot after him. His shoulder struck a trash can and it clattered to the sidewalk.

A large shadow filled the doorway. Mrs. La Gloria, her hair pulled back tightly against her head, her round short body squared off by a straight white coat, threw up her hands and rushed into the street.

"Here, kitty, kitty!" she called. Swinging her arms she slowed down, and turned to the customer

who had followed her from the doorway. "Leon," she said to Tenny's father, "I saw a coyote!" Her mouth hung open as she rubbed her arms and studied Leon's dark face to see if he thought her crazy. "I know I did!" she went on, encouraged by his silence. "I grew up in California. We'd see them come into the edge of town all the time." She turned and hustled along the sidewalk.

Leon nervously rustled his package as he watched the frenzied little lady hunt behind cans and boxes. His eyebrows puckered as he tried to make sense of the afternoon.

It had all begun in the pilot house when the chief engineer had told him to get rid of Tako. An argument had ensued. It had dragged on most of the afternoon, ending abruptly when Leon, realizing Tenny had not come to meet him, rushed to the deck in anger. She was nowhere around, but seeing the cage he decided to carry the coyote to the pet store. He thundered over to it. The cage door was open, the coyote gone. Furious, he picked it up and hurled it onto the deck. It rolled, bounced, then skidded under the rail, toppled, and dropped out of sight. As it splashed in the water below, Cardy Evans stepped aboard. Leon watched him come toward the pilot house. He was surveying the deck as he walked, obviously looking for something. Leon chuckled to himself, knowing full well why his friend was on the ship—somehow he'd gotten wind of the coyote. He was suddenly pleased. Cardy would have no satisfaction today.

Suspecting that Tako was safely hidden on the ship or in the warehouse, Leon became terribly helpful. "Coyote?" he said when questioned. "Well, now, let's look and see." They searched the ship with no results.

"Sorry," Cardy finally said. "Just a rumor I had to check."

Leon saw him off with a profusion of nice words. Now the fact that Tenny had not showed up pleased Leon. He wouldn't have to go home. He'd have time to find Tako; and so he spent the late afternoon and early evening looking behind wire coils and boxes, pulling aside crates and kicking coils of line. Finally he started off to rent a live trap. He never got to the hardware store, however, for he met an old friend along the way and they dropped into a favorite bar. It was ten o'clock before Leon started home with a plan to trap Tako at dawn. Thinking and scheming he stepped into Mrs. La Gloria's store for cigarettes and Italian sausage.

And now this!

Leon was frightened. Evans had made it clear that it was illegal to bring a wild animal into town without notification and a period of quarantine. There were fines for an offense. Fines worried him.

As he stood on the sidewalk he thought it best to forget the coyote. The animal was gone, the men on the ship hadn't talked, and so, hands crumpling his bag, Leon decided to delude Mrs. La Gloria and end the whole episode. She was impulsive, talkative, and persistent. Furthermore she probably *had* seen something. Leon strode toward her. She heard him coming and waited.

"I know a coyote when I see one!" she repeated violently.

Leon gazed dramatically down the street. "There! there! I see it."

Mrs. La Gloria leaned to the right. "Where?"

"Right there, by the can. See? It's a police dog. See it?"

"No."

"That's Towser," Leon insisted. "He belongs to a friend of mine. Guess I'll git 'im and take him home." He hurried to the shadows, scrambled the cans noisily, and finally shouted, "Got him," picked up a box, and strode off.

"I saw a coyote!" she called. "I ain't crazy." Then she paused. "At least I think I ain't." Her voice lowered. She shrugged. "Oh, well," she mumbled to herself, "can't do no more harm than the rats." She walked slowly to the store as another customer approached.

Tako had chased Rancid onto the carved stonework above the door of the Ceramic Tile Company, and then, at the sound of Mrs. La Gloria's shrilling, had dived over boxes and debris into the shadows. He knew an enemy when he heard one. He jumped down a pair of steps into the cellar well of the tile company, saw a broken slat in the door, and slipped into the dark basement. There he crouched and twisted his ears like antennae to keep tuned to the street. Suddenly he lifted his head. He listened. The sound of Leon's familiar step beat along the sidewalk above him. Tako slipped behind a shipping crate and lay still.

He did not come out of the basement until around two o'clock. The city was quiet. A few cabs cruised the streets, late buses drifted down the avenues. He tasted the wind. The scent of earth, stronger and cleaner now, excited him into a run. He held his nose low as he sped, for on the sidewalk under the trails of dogs, cats, and men, lay the faint odor of Tenny.

Tako streaked forward, his tawny fur waving beneath his belly, his tail low and curled. He passed under the railroad bridge, paused to smell a waste basket with a message from a pampered and neurotic dog, then shot on. He came to number 35. He stopped. Tenny's scent was strong here. It permeated the steps and stones, it mingled with other young human scents, and finally with Leon's.

Tako checked the smells again, and sensed their meaning. He had found Tenny's den. As he circled before the door the green wind gusted, drew him down the steps and on toward the switching limbs and leaves.

Tako's whole body focused on the trees. His tail straightened, his eyes did not shift. Gathering speed and moving with incredible grace, he crossed Fifth Avenue, pulled his feet up under him, and sailed like a winged dancer over the stone wall and into Central Park.

The Territory

Later in the morning, when it was again fully day, Tako peered out between the old stems of a ground-rambling rose that ceilinged in leaves and flowers above his head. He was in a formal garden. Petunias and begonias bloomed in tidy beds beyond the roses, and fat pigeons cooed to each other beside a fountain of dancing Graces. He stretched his toes and put his head down on his front paws. With ears and nose he catalogued the benefits that had come to him with one leap into Central Park. A squirrel chittered in a crab apple tree nearby, a robin sang from a gingko. Starlings cackled in the hedges of quince and far off a yellow-shafted flicker "wickered." The bubble of a house wren soothed him. These were comforting sounds to a coyote who had tuned in so long to the boom of men and boats and mechanical throbs. He pressed to the edge of the roses and looked across the flagstone walk to a wooded hill. He smelt the scent of lake water.

Tako lifted his head and peered upward. Somewhere above he heard the cry of a peregrin falcon. He sighted in on the sound and saw, high above the city, the pointed wings and blunt head of the duck hawk. The falcon closed her wings and dove, growing bigger as she plunged toward Central Park and Tako's formal garden. There was a burst of feathers beside the fountain and a pigeon lay beneath the yellow talons. Tako moved, the falcon saw him, covered her prey with her wings, took a triangulation on the top of the city, and rose heavily over the garden, the wall, and Fifth Avenue to the roof of the Museum of the City of New York.

Tako felt hungry. The smell of the dead bird had whetted his appetite, and he, too, eyed the pigeons now flying in a tight, frightened flock this way and that. They would not alight, however, for the falcon had triggered them into panic.

Tako surveyed the fountain. Sparrows were dropping beneath it. They fought and chirped. The coyote slipped out of the roses, pressed low through the petunias, and wedged to the edge of the garden. He lay under massive clumps of chrysanthemums as he judged which bird to snatch. Vibrations on the ground startled him. A gardener, dressed in the green uniform of the city Parks Department, was coming down the walk. He limped to the petunias, slowly got to his knees, and began to weed the red and blue flowers. His hair was gray at the temples and cut close to his head. He was short and round and his jowls drooped like a hound's as he worked. He was blue-eyed and gold like the earth.

Suddenly the sparrows chirped and bombed away. Tako watched them depart. Then he realized the flight of the birds was a warning. It was provoked by a sound he had missed. He recorded the image of flying sparrows preceding danger. They were more attuned to the city than he. An elderly woman, neatly dressed in dark clothing and shod in hard leather shoes, was coming down the path toward him. Her face was pink under her small neat hat, her frail hands were carefully gloved. She carried a brown paper bag.

"Good morning, Mr. Hansen," she said to the gardener, her voice steady and bright.

"Good morning, Miss Landry," the gardener answered, rising and holding his hip. "It's a good mornin' for flowers and birds, but not for me." He rubbed his leg. "It must be goin' to rain. I'm stiff as a rake prong."

Tako threw up his ears as Miss Landry's bag rustled and sounds of falling bread tattooed the walk. The sparrows came flying back. Two fluttered into the chrysanthemums as they fought over a piece of bread. Beating their wings and jabbing with their feet, they whirled to the ground not a foot from his mouth. Tako arched his back, sprang upon one, and slid back to the shelter of roses.

Miss Landry clutched Mr. Hansen's arm. "What was that?" she asked quickly. "There!" She pointed.

The gardener parted the flowers. "I don't see nothin'," he said unconvincingly. He did not wish to alarm a bird lover.

"Did anything get loose from the zoo?" Miss Landry asked. "It looked like a wolf."

"Now, now, Miss Landry," the gardener said. "I'da heard about that at the park house! It's just the wind in the bushes."

Miss Landry walked around the fountain. The birds were now coming in flocks from all parts of the park. She tossed bread, looked into hedges, and, still not convinced, glanced at the gardener. He was staring into the roses. He turned, met her gaze, and smiled. "Wind," he said, "a little whirlwind of leaves."

Miss Landry finished feeding the birds, picked off a few dead flowers, and departed—erect and on schedule. The sun was touching the tops of the skyscrapers on Central Park West, her time to go home. When she had tapped away, Mr. Hansen hurried to the chrysanthemums and got down on his knees. A red stain of blood colored the ground

and beside it lay a wing feather. But there was no bird. He weaved as he searched the petunias and the roses. It wasn't no wolf, he mused to himself, but it wasn't no dog, either.

Tako, deep in the rose tangles, never took his eyes off Mr. Hansen. The man was hunting. Tako sensed this from the aggressive stance and he crouched, ready to flee.

But the gardener got to his feet, turned his back, and went off to the iris bed. Tako worked his way through the roses to the far edge of the garden. He crossed the sidewalk, leaped into the English ivy under the crab apple tree orchard, and trotted into a flowering hedge. Then he dashed down a flagstone walk, passed the brick tool house, and darted up grass steps into an arbor of wisteria. Sliding through this he found himself at the edge of the woods. He ran freely up the hill and stopped above the glassy water of Harlem Meer. It was silver in the early morning. Glancing back at the gardener, Tako went on, in the manner of all young animals seeking a territory of their own. If one spot relays a sense of pressure the wanderer looks further. The hunting eyes of Mr. Hansen were uncomfortable. Instinctively Tako moved away.

He trotted under trees, around bushes, over footpaths on his way to the lake. The water was low, dirty, and varnished with scum. There would be no herons or frogs at its edges nor would the exposed banks make a good home site. He sauntered westward, listening casually to the surrounding city. It stridulated like an insect chorus as cars converged and the daylight work of men brought clangor to the morning. Tako was not alarmed. These mechanical sounds of man had remained confined to streets and buildings since he had first heard them. Being an animal of habit himself, he sensed these were the trails of the people. He felt secure.

He noticed other matters of coyote concern. The earth between the trees was pounded hard by feet, and the wildflowers had been replaced by papers, cans, and bottles. One bottle smelled sweet. Tako tipped it with his paw, spinning the word "Coke" into view. It dripped and he tasted its contents. It was pleasant. Licking his jowls he pushed his tongue into the bottle for more. It stuck. Tako pulled to get it out. It stuck tighter. Then with canny presence he relaxed and his tongue slid out. He dashed away. He would avoid bottles. This had been an unsuccessful experience and Tako learned from failure as well as success.

Trotting and running, he climbed a rock ledge

and came upon a road. A cascade of cars poured along it, so he retreated under a low-lying yew tree to judge his next move. Suddenly a blue jay announced him. Then predictably, another got the word and screamed, too. A crow, gleaning sparkling treasures at a trash basket some hundred yards away, heard the "enemy" cry and hopped on her wings to come and harass—a pastime far better for a crow than picking aluminum foil and strings from a basket. She set up such a persistent clacket that Tako moved under a copse of ivy. The jay still dove at him. He snapped at it, moving his ears constantly, in the expectation that the people would be attracted to the commotion. No footsteps fell. He smelled each wind. They carried no stalking human scents and so it was printed on his mind once more that people did not understand animals. Nevertheless Tako felt rawly conspicuous. So clear was the bird language to him, so vividly did they declare "enemy," that he dug into the earth until the birds, with their short memories, forgot him and flew away. It was a tense wait although not a man arrived.

Eventually the flow of traffic thinned and Tako saw an opportunity to cross to the denser and wilder woods on the other side of the road. He dashed just as a mounted policeman rounded the bend. The horse saw Tako, shied, and whinnied. The coyote zigzagged into the grass and shot up the hill like a rifle bullet. He sped down a ravine where a gray stream splashed out of the pool, trickled under a wooden foot bridge, and seeped into the Loch. The trees of the ravine were dense, and the protective underbrush of wood nettles and raspberries enveloped him. He stopped behind an oak tree and looked far down the hill to the man. Again, the speech of animals went unheard. The policeman's head was lowered as he tried to calm his frightened horse.

Tako forgot them. His attention was riveted on a clump of spreading laurel. He pounced beneath it. His paws sunk into the earth, and he began digging with the urgency of a coyote long deprived of home and shelter.

When he had a hollow deep enough to hide himself he kicked leaves into it and lay down. Instantly he was asleep, for he had not rested completely since the last day on the freighter.

He did not sleep long. A red-eyed vireo dropped limb by limb from the high canopy of the trees and clicked at him. He glanced up, for the vireo had alarmed the birds that lived in the tops of the trees, and two orioles and a yellow warbler had joined the scolding session.

Tako got to his feet. He yawned in boredom at the frightened birds and stretched. Now that he was awake he felt restless. He must wander. His survival depended on knowledge of his territory and so, despite his weariness, he was driven on. He took a wooded path that led to an open meadow. Standing in patches of sunlight and shadow he observed the gray caps and clothing of a team of young baseball players. He sat down and curiously watched them throw a ball to each other, bat it, run, and stop.

Although he did not understand their activity, he sensed it was play. He and his sisters had often tossed and flipped mice to each other with the same exuberance. He watched the game with interest, then slipped through the brush and took the sheltered edge of the bridle path to the other side of the lawn.

There he raised his head and listened with his keen ears. Far away a piping tinkle of music sounded. It brought no images, no pictures or reactions to his mind. It just sparkled on, underscored by the faint squeal of children. Tako's curiosity glowed. He started off to investigate the music

maker on his territory of Central Park. The digging
of his den had satisfied his need for a home. Now
he must defend it in the manner of all home own-
ers. The carousel, circling to the music of the calliope, sounded alive, and Tako trotted around the
edge of the North Meadow to judge whether or not
it was a threat.

It was night when he got back to his den. He had
never reached the carousel for along the way he
met a female German shepherd, an aggressive bitch
her master called Poovey.

The meeting had been cyclonic. Tako was swinging along the bridle path that encircled the Reservoir. The body of water was fenced from him and
therefore unattainable, but he could smell sea gulls
rafting upon it, and robins at its edges. Then he
trotted over a bridge across 86th Street's transverse
road, glancing down into the traffic as he crossed.
He paused briefly to watch the cars pass below,
then loped into another woodland. Among the trees
a playground of romping children sent him into the
bushes again. He came out on a ramblers' path behind the Metropolitan Museum of Art and swung
elegantly down the center of the deserted trail. He
was feeling kinglike, taking stock of sights and
sounds on the shadowed trail when out of a down

wind the shepherd lunged, taking him by surprise. Snapping the leash from her master's hand, she bore down on Tako. Dirt flying, she almost struck him before he sensed she was attacking. Usually males and females do not clash, but Poovey was trail-sensitive. Tako was on her territory. He darted into the underbrush, wove into leafy cover, then started north at a dead heat. He easily outdistanced her.

At an inner signal, he turned and waited for the bitch. He would not yield the land he had explored this morning. He charged her. She bristled her neck, barked, and turned back. She understood. The fight was over, the arrangement made. Tako's land lay to the north of the Great Lawn, Poovey's to the south.

Dragging her leash, the shepherd trotted down the bridle path. A young man's voice shouted angrily, "Poovey, what's the matter with you? Heel! Poovey, heel!" Tako did not wait to learn any more. A vibration on the ground told him a horse was approaching, and a sniff relayed the fact she was mounted. He slipped into a ground cover of honeysuckle and lay down. As the horse came upon Tako's trail she shied and whinnied, but Tako was not afraid this time. Her announcement, he knew, would make no impression on the man. When the officer had the mare under control, he grumbled, "That's the second time you've spooked today. What's goin' on, Lady Ann?" He patted her neck and shoulder. She steadied and trotted away.

As Tako wandered home he investigated the Shakespeare Garden from its hedges and the wading pool from a bush. Everywhere endless lines of park benches were splattered with messages from dogs of all ages, dominance, and subdominance. Finally, with nose, eyes, and ears, he filled in the details of his territory. There were also birds, mice, rats, snakes, and insects. Cats slinked in the shadows.

Upon his return to his den he was satisfied that Central Park was good coyote territory.

The stars were only faint sparks above the city gleam as he put his nose in his tail. He had no sooner dropped off to sleep than a heaving rumble sounded in the earth. It roared to a climax and died like a thunder roll. He got up to investigate but was diverted by a trembling movement in the leaves nearby. He recognized the odor and whiskers of a brown rat testing the night before she dared to venture. Tako watched her; and, in the manner of his father and his breed, he did not pounce on her. His harvest would take place at greater distances from his den. Reserves were important to his sense of well-being.

The rat came out of her burrow under an oak root and trembled as she glanced around almost blindly for others of her kind. There were so many rats in the city and the fight for survival was so intense that the beasts feared each other more than they feared men. Satisfied that she was alone, she hurried down her trail, a narrow groove, trampled into the earth by her many trips to and from her home. Tako stepped softly and followed her. She went up a hill and around a rock. There she paused to let another rat she had sensed a few yards in front of her put distance between them. She waited with stiffened whiskers and a rigid tail—a pose of defense. Then she hurried on.

She crossed a sidewalk, went under a bench, and padded swiftly to a large iron grille. Gradually the thunder roll began again, louder and more vibrant than before. Tako drew back cautiously. The sound died ominously, but the rat, he noted, did not even slow her pace. Sensing that she was not frightened, he felt reassured. He sniffed the grating. Drafts of warm air gusted out, bringing the odor of oil and people. Once more he hesitated. Below the grating lay a dimly lighted room. He shied and glanced toward the rat to see her reaction. She had disappeared. He tracked her to a hole at the edge of the grating, dug by rats but enlarged by dogs. Tako pushed himself through and dropped down onto a narrow cement ledge. He moved along carefully. Far below, tracks of steel shot horizontally under the earth, odd electric odors hovered over them, and they snapped with unknown but nonliving sounds. Tako looked for the rat. She was far ahead, running swiftly toward the room of light.

He hurried now. Tunnels in the earth were part of his desert memory, and having taken stock of the inanimate subway he began to feel secure beneath the city. The rat halted, stood up on her hind feet, and thrust her nose into a trickle of glittering water. She drank from a pipe. It had been chewed open by generations of rats passing in the night. Tako waited until she had moved on, then he slid forward and drank also, little knowing that he was helping himself to the city water supply.

The thunder started again, louder and more terrifying than before. Suddenly a subway train sped out of the darkness and screamed through the tunnel below. Tako hugged the wall as the cement foundation trembled and the earth shook. The train came to a stop. People emerged from it. Others disappeared into it. Bells clanged, doors slammed, and the train moved, gathered momentum, and sped off into the dark. Tako watched its lights grow smaller, then disappear around a bend. When it was gone he relaxed, noticing that the rat had not stopped for its thunderous passing. She was leaping down great blocks of cement to another ledge. Tako balanced himself and jumped after her. He followed her to the subway platform where several rats were burrowing through papers, leaping into

trash containers, and snatching chewing gum wrappers off the floor. Occasionally they got too close to each other and fought violently.

Tako examined their loot. It was of little interest to him and so he surveyed this new country. Walls gleamed white, lights burned, tunnels led off tunnels. He trotted down the platform, found stairs, loped up them and rounded a corner. At the top of the next stairs the jagged silver skyline of the city was framed in the square subway entrance. Gingerly he climbed until he was looking down Central Park West. The avenue shone more brilliantly than the stars above the desert and rumbled with sounds of automobiles. It smelled of dry cement.

Tako registered the avenue in his mind—a canyon of a million lights and movements. Beads of color rose up the walls and lit the haze. Startled by the brilliance Tako moved against the fence of the park and concentrated all his senses upon the night city.

Down the street stood the Museum of Natural History, which, unknown to him, had an exhibit of coyotes on the main floor. The legend under the stuffed animals read: "Coyote (Brush wolf) *Canis latrans*. The coyote seeks irregular terrain with open fields, bushy edges and woodland. It is at home in the deserts and mountains. Curiosity is one of its traits. It has a high degree of 'native intelligence' and is faster than a dog when running. On its home range of several hundred acres, the coyote often passes up food near the den and hunts far afield.

"The den is approached by a circuitous route. About three quarters of the coyote's food is rodents and rabbits. Females begin breeding when two years old and gestation takes 63 days. Five to ten pups are born."

The legend went on: "The coyote has moved to the east and is now established in the Adirondacks and Catskills. He is highly adaptable and thrives in western cities. None, however, is in New York City. This is fortunate, for they bring in parasites and often breed with dogs like collies and shepherds."

Tako was listening to sparrows. They had awakened and were arguing over roosts in the illuminated night. He followed their voices around the subway entrance to a newsstand, a wooden building with its green windows drawn for the night. The birds were louder here. He looked up. Grass, newspaper, pins, and tin foil stuffed in the eaves of the building and an odor of oily dust told him he had nests on this part of his territory. He could not see the birds.

A low sound caught his attention. It began softly

and rose rhythmically. Music emanated from an open window across the avenue. The notes were strange but pleasant, almost as pleasant as a coyote chorus on the desert, but far less meaningful to him. The music did not speak of homes and territories and rollicking pups, but it touched this memory, and Tako felt desperately isolated and homesick. He drooped his head, his shoulder blades parted the fur on his back, and his tail hung low.

Suddenly the drum of heels aroused him. A man was hurrying toward the subway. Tako let him pass, then softly followed in his tracks, taking comfort from his animal warmth. The man walked head down, heard the train, and ran. He rushed down the steps. Tako followed him into the subway as the train drew up and stopped. Pausing under the turnstile, he watched the long line of cars suck open a dozen bright doors. The man stepped in, was closed off and carried away. When the train sped off Tako noticed another man. He had stepped out of the cars and was singing and weaving like a tumbleweed in the wind. As he started through the turnstile he noticed Tako. "Nishe doggie," he said slushily, and Tako sensed he was too frolicsome to be a threat. He was right; the man was merrily drunk and affectionately patted the coyote and rubbed his ears. The contact felt good to Tako and he reacted with a nudge. His loneliness vanished and he trotted off to defend his latest acquisition—the subway.

Returning to the ledge, he saw many rats running along the tracks. Others were departing, climbin the walls to other secret runways under the city. The coyote sauntered homeward. His homesickness had passed and a sense of pride in his rich territory dominated his spirit. He found his way back to the grating, emerged in the woods, and tacked home by a "circuitous route."

The route embraced the Block House, a stone rectangle on the highest hill of the park, the boat house at Harlem Meer, the formal garden, and, finally, the laurel bush. He came toward it from the north. Almost home, he was startled by an angry spitting above his head, drew back, and looked into the eyes of a striped house cat. The glance was only instantaneous; the cat sprang out of a tree and landed on Tako's head. Tako spun to the ground and tore out of her grip, snarling and snapping; but before he could retaliate with a bite, she had leaped back to the tree, climbed to a limb, and was hissing at him.

Tako dashed away. The tiger cat, he knew by

her scent, was a mother of kittens. He now sniffed them in the hole behind her. Well-trained, they did not cry, but the sweet odor of milk-fed young hung over the mother and the hollow. Knowing the violence of a mother cat defending her young he ran full pace.

As he slid under the laurel a robin opened its eyes. The bird sat in silence as it slowly came awake. Then it moved, flitting from twig to twig to the top of the tall red oak. There it chirped brightly, announcing the dawn to the other robins in the park. They answered back. The morning sang with bird talk.

Tako made himself comfortable as the duck hawk called pipingly above the city. She was riding up the thermal currents and peering down on the roof tops and parks in her daily hunting tour. The coyote slept as the city came awake.

Ice Cream

By the end of the week Tako had explored his territory from the southern edge of the Great Lawn to the wall at 110th Street and from Fifth Avenue to Central Park West. He knew where the pigeons roosted and the sparrows slept. He had carefully harvested several mice behind the gardener's tool shed, but, like a good plantation manager, had left enough to reproduce and raise more. Occasionally he tried to extend his territory to include the Lake where he heard and smelled ducks, but messages from Poovey shied him off. She had a menacing sense of possession and deposited sharp urine threats for Tako all along their boundary line. He stayed out of her land not because he was afraid of her, but because they had settled property rights, and, in the manner of the wild dog he was, he respected this.

One night around midnight Tako felt a need to recheck his original holdings—109th Street. He leaped over the wall, swept across Fifth Avenue, and took to the shadows along the corner building. As he neared number 35, he scented Tenny. She was sitting alone on the steps, her head against the doorway, her eyes on a window across the street where music vibrated and the Street Family danced and laughed. Tako slipped into an empty cardboard box lying on its side beside the trash can, and peered out at the girl.

She was singing to the beat. He cocked his ears. The sounds she made were vibrant, high, and birdlike. He was inspired to wail with her as he had in the desert when the coyotes sang, but fortunately was diverted by the smell of a cold sweetness that made his mouth salivate. Tenny was licking an ice-cream cone. Tako watched it, crept out of the box, and climbed on it to get nearer to the cone. His nose was close to Tenny's arm. She licked, then lowered her hand. The ice cream was available. He licked it. The taste was compelling. He watched

anxiously as her hand went back to her mouth. When it came down he took the whole thing.

Tenny gasped and pulled herself into a tense knot. She hugged her shoulders and looked down as Tako retreated into the box with the ice cream. It was sweetly devourable, but cold.

Tenny's feet tramped down the steps. She came toward him. "Tako!" she whispered. "Tako, where are you?" Her tone was warm. Tako swallowed the ice cream, then leaped to his feet. A cold pain moved down his throat. For an instant his head ached. The sweetness hurt violently until the ice cream melted and slid down to his stomach. Feeling better, he went back to the dessert, licked the box where the cone had fallen, and finally turned his attention to Tenny. She was peering anxiously into the dark box, but could not see him. She moved away and searched the trash.

"They know you're in the city, Tako," she cried softly. Her fingers flexed like a cat's paw. "Mr. Evans found the cage in the river. Where are you?" She ran a few steps toward the street. Tako finished the last crumbs of the cone and lay down. Tenny came back.

"He's looking real hard, Tako!" Her voice was tense. She ran around the steps. Her hands seemed to push back the dark. Once more she called his name.

To herself she said, Mr. Evans is terribly thorough. How do I warn a wild animal? Still searching for him she ran toward Fifth Avenue and, glancing to the right and left, turned the corner. "Tako," she called, "where are you?" She crossed into the park.

Tako shook his fur loose, stepped onto the sidewalk, and jogged toward the East River, not comprehending, not knowing why Tenny cried out.

Placing his feet to the rhythm of the music of the Street Family, he wended his way in and out of doorways to Park Avenue. There he stretched and judged the night.

It was late, most of the people had retired. Nevertheless, he traveled the next two blocks under cars. He wanted to avoid both man and beast. When he checked the fence at the river he turned back.

Halfway home he picked up a familiar scent. Rancid, Mrs. La Gloria's tomcat, was patrolling his property between Lexington and Third. Tako burst into a run. He was not hunting, he was not even protecting his territory. He was acting on impulse. Tako did not like Rancid.

The cat sensed him coming, turned quickly, and arched into a spindle of bristles. Tako plunged.

Rancid leaped to the left, climbed a flight of stairs, jumped to an urn, and sprang up into the night. He lit on the bottom rung of a fire escape ladder, balanced himself, and rocketed into the darkness.

Tako followed to the top of the stairs. He studied the ladder, then, drawing upon his skill on rocks and ledges, he leaped after Rancid. He leaped high, came down on the first landing of the fire escape, picked up the frightened tom's scent, and sped upward. His feet touched the steps twice as he took a corner and raced up the next flight. The cat was gliding ahead of him.

At the third landing Tako hesitated. A light shone through the windows on the top floor. People's voices crackled. He stole toward them. In a brightly lit room he saw a man and a woman. They moved slowly in the circling manner he himself used before bedding down. Tako ducked under the window light, and glided to the next iron staircase. The people talked lazily.

"I've gotta change the water on the pigeons," the man grumbled. "I don't feel like it."

"Yaa," the woman mumbled. "Well, I tell you one thing, Herb, I ain't gonna do it." Her voice was irritated.

"I didn't ask you to," Herb shouted and got to his

feet. He strode toward the door. "Where's the flash-light? I nearly broke my neck on a pipe last night 'cause I couldn't find it."

"How do I know?" grumbled the woman from the bathroom as she turned water into the sink. "Why don't you get rid of those birds? You're always complainin' about 'em."

" 'Cause you like the money when they win races!" he shouted and stormed out of the door.

Their angry bickering floated meaninglessly past Tako. He rounded the steps and climbed to the roof where Rancid's scent was strong.

For a moment he hesitated on the top of the par-apet that walled off the flat building top. He looked down on the city. Chains of light ran like rivers down buildings and over streets. The sky was lit with particles of smog that held the city in a halo. Miles of squares and rectangles piled up for as far as he could see. Tako swayed in pleasure. An old memory flashed over him. He was high on a hill in the live oak forest with his father, the moon was lighting the dust in the air, and the coyotes were wailing.

Tako straightened his forelegs and took a broad stance with his hind ones. Then he threw back his head and wailed. His voice rolled out over the city.

It pierced the sounds of buses and subways, it wound higher than the cry of a child. Rancid was forgotten as Tako chilled himself with his own glorious song of well-being.

A thud and the scratching of claws ended his serenade. He turned and saw the terrified cat sliding off the roof of a bulky, round water tower. Tako stood still, judging where the cat would fall.

Then he caught another movement. Pigeons, awakened by his eerie cry, fluttered wildly inside a tall cage. He leaped off the parapet and alighted

below them. Sniffing and licking his jowls, he circled the cage. The birds were cut off from him by a
mesh of chicken wire. He paid no heed to their
wheeling flights of panic for he was concentrating
on a way in to them. They were sweet smelling and
seed-fed, unlike the scavenger pigeons of the city
that ate anything. Near the rear of the cage he saw
that the wire buckled. He got his teeth in it, and
yanked until the wire squealed and stretched.

At this moment the roof door to the building
opened. The man he had seen in the room below
appeared. Tako dropped to his belly and studied
him. Herb fumbled in the dark and Tako slid behind the cupola in the time it took for the man's
eyes to adjust to the dark.

Then Rancid lost his grip on the water tower and
dropped, squealing, onto the top of the pigeon
cage. The birds flopped and beat their wings. Herb
dashed to the cage, saw the cat, and took off a
shoe. As Rancid leaped to the roof top, the man
hurled the shoe. He shouted in anger. Tako stayed
behind the cupola until the skirmish was over, the
birds watered, and the trumpeting Herb safe within the building.

Then he went back to the wire and yanked at it
again. When he had torn a small hole he widened

it with his nose, his head, and then his shoulders. Silently he slipped into the cage. He easily caught a wheeling bird, squeezed out, and carried it to the side of the chimney.

After finishing his meal he stood up, shook himself, and licked his chest until the fur sparkled. Then he leaped gracefully to the parapet, looked down on the city once more, and listened to the wind turn shrill square corners around buildings and streets. Finally he walked down the fire escape, not pausing at the lighted window even though Herb shouted fiercely, ". . . and I'll get that Mrs. La Gloria's cat if it's the last thing I do."

On the bottom landing Tako lifted his head, sniffed the street for danger, then leaped to the ground and trotted back toward Central Park. As he passed number 35, he checked the steps briefly. Tenny was inside. He walked on jauntily. On the sidewalk near the corner he smelled the scent of anger. Tenny had met Elaine here. Their encounter had been intense, but of little interest to a well-fed coyote. He walked to the curb, waited for a taxi to pass down Fifth Avenue, then crossed and leaped over the wall. He trotted south between the wall and the fence of a play area. It was late and he was tired, and observing that the park was deserted he took an easier trail—the middle of the walk. At the formal garden he circled the chrysanthemums that were softly snapping as they grew in the dark, and slipped under the cover of rambler roses.

When the sun was shining again, he heard Mr. Hansen come to work. Tako did not move, for something about the little square man with his earthy movements inspired trust. So Tako rested, listening to the clink of Mr. Hansen's trowel striking pebbles and stones. Then came the tap of Miss Landry's hard wide heels as she entered the park through the wrought-iron gates at 107th Street. She clicked down the spacious steps to the wisteria garden and turned right. Louder now, her steps approached the splashing fountain. Her paper bag rustled familiarly, and, as always, she spoke to Mr. Hansen. The birds arrived from all over the park, and presently the heels tapped off and died away.

Tako yawned and peered through the roses. Having rested, he now had an urge to wander. He waited for the trowel to clatter, indicating that the gardener was occupied, then stepped onto the walk. He trotted a few steps, sensed eyes were upon him and glanced back to see Mr. Hansen standing erect and staring. Slowly the man smiled.

Tako felt no need to hide. He walked on casually.

At the tool house he came upon a truck parked on the wide walk. The open rear end was loaded with baskets, flats of plants, and tools. He was about to go around it, when on the walk of the wisteria garden appeared a woman and three leashed dogs. They were coming his way. Sensing a conflict, Tako slipped under the truck and crawled up onto the differential.

The dogs passed without picking up his scent. They were yapping and shouldering each other. People began to arrive, ladies from the nursing home across the street, old men from Fifth Avenue apartments, and children with nurses. Tako stayed where he was.

Mr. Hansen approached the truck. He threw his tools in the rear, got in the cab, and started the engine. Before Tako could make a stay-or-flee decision, the car was moving slowly down the walk to the road. He tried to see where he was going, but only the hard roadbed and the bottoms of the trees were visible.

Presently he smelled the cool air from the reservoir, and next the warm grass-wind from the ball field. Then the truck rolled over the border that he and Poovey had settled upon, and stopped at the

Sheep Meadow where the New York Philharmonic Symphony played evening concerts under the stars. Mr. Hansen got out, took out a flat of flowers, and limped toward the orchestra shell.

Tako climbed down from the iron shaft and lay under the truck. He surveyed the new land. Paths and benches, bushes and trees encircled the open meadow. Bicycles passed on meandering trails and spangled horse-drawn hansoms wheeled slowly down the road. Faintly on the wind came the odor of food—hamburgers, cheeses, eggs—salivatory scents from the larders of people.

Tako saw a bushy hedge several feet away. He dashed into it, and moved inconspicuously to the edge of the Mall. A large fountain erupted into the sky and fell back into a stone-lined pool. Beyond the pool lay the lake where Tako had smelled the ducks, so long locked off from him by Poovey's threats. But that was not what absorbed his interest now. The café on the Mall was far more inviting. Under canopies of stripes stood tables laden with the scents he had smelled earlier. Popcorn and spicy hot dogs challenged his nose. Tako's mouth dripped streams of water as he calculated how to tackle the tables that were surrounded by people. He tried a circuitous route to the statuary at the bottom of the Mall steps. There were people here. He could not cross.

He glanced at the sculpture carved on either side of the steps. Among stone bodies of fish, men, and mermaids were cavities and holes. Tako leaped up onto a giant leg, crept into a sea shell, and wedged into a mermaid's arm. He leaped to a fish head, slipped down behind it, and came out on a dolphin fin. He had crossed the promenade. The woods and the other side of the café lay ahead. With a rush he dove under a weeping beech and faced the aromatic steam table. It was inaccessible. People were everywhere. Tako lay down to await darkness, when laughter and a familiar sweet odor behind him attracted his attention. He wove through an alder hedge to the edge of a circle that surrounded the tall statue of Hans Christian Andersen. It was laden with climbing children, but Tako was not concerned with the play of young human beings; he was watching a man with a white cart, who was handing out something that he had come to crave —ice cream. One small child, who Tako understood from his wobbly movements was no more than a weaned pup, teetered away from the adult he was with and wove toward the alders. He carried dripping brown and white ice cream on a stick. Tako kept his eyes on the delicacy and the wobbly hand, until, as he anticipated, the child lost his balance and went down on all fours. The ice cream hit with a soft splash two feet away. Tako wiggled forward and licked the ice cream. The child balanced himself and slowly rose. He saw Tako and sat down. His laughter was like tail wagging. Tako listened, licked, and kept the top of his eyes on the child. The child stared.

The other children began to come together into a pattern. They drifted over to the statue and sat down in a circle. Their backs were to Tako. The little boy before him, however, did not join them. He was totally absorbed in Tako. Presently he reached out and patted him, wiggled closer, bent over, and peered into his mouth. Tako sensed his innocence and neither growled nor pulled away. The child's movements and odors were completely unaggressive. Tako continued to lick, being careful not to gulp and feel cold pain again. Suddenly a shrill call of alarm, like the hysterical cries of the jays and the crows, told him to retreat. "Andy! Andy!" a nurse screamed. She was weaving through the children. Upon seeing her charge, she dashed to his side. The child laughed and pointed into the hedge, but the woman did not look. She only

picked him up and brushed him off. She cleaned his chin and as he reached for the ice cream she slapped his hand.

"Dirty, dirty." Her voice was filled with warning sounds. "I'll get you another."

She led him off. Tako waited. The circling group was now quiet. Then a woman from the Children's Department of the New York Public Library stood up before the bronze sculpture, and the eyes of the children and adults concentrated upon her. Tako slid forward and licked the last of the ice cream, pulled back into the leaves, and watched for other careless puppies as the woman began to speak. "Once upon a time," she said gently, "a long time ago, there was a pretty girl named Little Red Riding Hood."

No more ice cream came his way. Tako put his head on his paws and fell asleep to the make-believe story of a wolf and a child.

When he awoke, the rays of the August sun had folded the leaves on the hedge and were filtering down upon him hot and dry. The children were gone. Carefully he retraced his steps to the South Lawn. Mr. Hansen and the truck had vanished.

Tako assessed his environment. Sensitive now to the rise and fall of the city life, he had become aware of a pause in the park around six o'clock. Yet this evening was different. People were assembling. They were moving into the Sheep Meadow. Some sat down, some stretched out on their backs. Others ate, and the odors of hot dogs, tuna fish, bread, and cakes surrounded them. Once more Tako calculated how to obtain this food. He left the hedge, wedged through a grove of mountain ash, and worked his way to the rocky hill above the meadow and into a shadowy grove of ironwood and alder. As Tako searched for a spot to watch the people he smelled a garter snake in the cracks of the rocks. The snake thrust out its tongue, tasted Tako on the wind, and slid away. The coyote took over his bed, for it was a well-protected place in deep cover.

He did not relax. Head on his paws, eyes on the lawn below, Tako studied the people. Their movements were casual and languid. They ate and spoke. Their pups played and wrestled. He sensed their well-being and stretched out on his side, patiently waiting for an opportunity to share their food.

As the twilight descended, expectancy tightened the assembly of people. They talked more and moved less. Then men gathered in the orchestra shell, took gleaming instruments out of cases, and sat down. The enormous crowd in the meadow came to attention. Silky sounds rose from the shell and to the amazement of the coyote the twilight filled with winds of music. Tako stood up, threw his head back, and sang with the New York Philharmonic.

To the south of him a dog barked. From the woods behind came the caterwaul of the tiger cat. Tako wailed again. The people on the edge of the meadow stirred and glanced into the woods. Then they looked away, as lightly through the air came the measures of Beethoven's Sixth Symphony. Tako put his head down. The dog stopped barking, the cat was silent, and Tako was utterly still.

Footsteps alerted him. He spun his ears. Someone was coming toward him. He jumped to his feet. The wind brought the scent of Tenny. She had left her blanket, placed near José, Elaine, Maria, and two other members of the Street Family, had slipped through the crowd, and was climbing the rocks.

Tako watched her move in the dark. She stumbled and felt around with her hands. At the top of the rock, climbing now on all fours, she scanned the dark woods. Tako stared at her but saw that she did not see him. Her eyes passed over him twice.

"Tako!" she whispered. The voice was gentle but worried. The same confidence she had given him the first day they met she imparted now. He moved toward her. "Tako!" The music romped on. Tako moved closer. Tenny paused, not sure which way to go. Tako felt pleasure. He pranced. He stirred the leaves. Tenny swung around and stared. Tako cavorted in a circle around her. She still did not see him; but she knew he was there, for she drew up and shivered with the eerie sensation of being seen, but not seeing.

Tako nudged her hand. She reached down and touched his back.

"Tako!" Her voice trembled. "How can I tell you to hush up? They're still hunting you. They think you're down by the river." She stooped and held out her hand blindly. "Here! Eat this and be quiet." Tako smelled a tangy pizza and came so close that even in the dark Tenny could see him. She smiled and her black eyes twinkled. "No, no," she said. "Don't wail!" Tako felt the pleasure of her companionship, snatched the food, and skittered off into the woods in a wide circle. He sped back still holding the pizza, but Tenny was stumbling down the rocks. He watched her wind into the vast crowd.

The Street Family also watched her. Elaine rose

and stepped around people to meet her. "Where've ya been?" she asked sweetly.

"Wheredya think?" Tenny answered curtly and sat down.

"Don't kid me," Elaine said. "I heard a coyote. Mrs. La Gloria's right."

"Ridiculous," Tenny answered.

"You went to see him, didn'ya, Tenny?" Elaine persisted.

"I went to the ladies' room."

"Wait'll I tell Maria's Mom. She's helping Mr. Evans, you know. She saw him."

"Please be quiet, Elaine. I'm listening."

Elaine pushed her red curls out of her eyes and picked her way back toward the Street Family. She tapped José's shoulder. "That *was* a coyote. And Tenny *does* know something. I can tell. I've known her for a long time."

José stretched his neck and looked over the heads toward the girl. "Thought you said she was too good to be real. Couldn't be . . . Still . . ." He rubbed the back of his head. "It was her father's freighter."

The music swept toward the finale. Then the whole orchestra took the last note and held it softly. The audience was silent.

From the hill behind another note began, wa-

vered, trilled higher and higher, and stopped on a tremulous wail. Heads turned, there was some nervous laughter and then the whole eerie instant was drowned in a thunder of applause.

Maria stood up and glanced at Tenny. It seemed to her, even in the dark, that Tenny looked frightened. She whispered to José, "Tenny's scared. She *did* let him go." Then she laughed. "Tenny," she repeated. "Tenny, the funny one who wanted to do kind deeds."

José wrinkled his brows and pondered. His bronze hands clapped more and more slowly. Finally they stopped altogether and he turned to

Broni. Broni was a sort of wall off whom José bounced ideas.

"This Tenny," he said. "She's a bit unusual, but anyone who sets a coyote loose right under the eyes of cops, health inspectors, and her old man can't be too bad; and she may need some friends."

Broni turned an expressionless face on José.

"So?"

"So it's time to call another membership meeting, don'tcha think?"

Broni nodded. José began clapping again. His eyes sparked as he glanced back into the woods and then down at the dusky young girl who stood by herself among thousands.

Downtown and Uptown

September blew in cold. The blackbirds flocked in the meadow and the swallows circled the city. Butterfly wings tore in the wind and the fragile insects crept under the leaves and flowers to die in a dream, their eggs laid close beside on twigs and bark to carry on the life that was gone.

Tako left his laurel den around four one morning, traipsed across the empty road and around Harlem Meer. He noted the ducks that had dropped in on migration. He did not chase them, however, for he was on his way to the formal garden to catch a fat pigeon and find the truck that had carried him so successfully across Poovey's trail.

He arrived before Mr. Hansen or Miss Landry, circled the fountain, and caught a sleeping bird in the hedge of flowering quince. He consumed it where he had caught it, then swayed grandly down the wide walk to the tool house. It was locked for the night; but a message from a dog lay blatantly against the door. "I've passed," the urine asserted. Tako nullified it with his own scent of possession and dominance—"I own this territory," he replied. Satisfied that he had intimidated the dog that must travel on a leash and never really possess Central Park, he slipped into the crab apple garden and lay down in the ivy. The falcon called above the Fifth Avenue buildings, then dropped beside the fountain. Tako heard death—to him a sound of harvesting and the continuation of life.

Other sounds of morning arose—the footsteps of Mr. Hansen, then Miss Landry, the rattle of her paper bag, the flick of bird wings. Tako heard the ticking rhythm of a new day in the park with such lazy pleasure that he almost missed his ride across Poovey's line. Mr. Hansen was starting the truck.

Fortunately, the gardener was interrupted by Miss Landry, who tapped on his door and called,

"Yoo, hoo!" and while Mr. Hansen leaned across the front seat and rolled down the window Tako walked to the rear of the truck and climbed up on the differential. He could not hear the conversation for the roar of the motor, but it concerned him.

"Mr. Hansen," Miss Landry began. "Remember the wolf I thought I saw several weeks ago?" Mr. Hansen nodded. "One of my friends who goes to the Philharmonic concerts, and who ought to know, said she heard a coyote in the park." Mr. Hansen cupped his hand to his ear. "Yes?" he said. "Go on."

"Well, I told her that if anybody knew anything about a coyote in Central Park that you certainly would because you're digging around in it all the time."

"I certainly would," he said and winked. Miss Landry understood and squeezed her gloved hands excitedly. "I thought so." She turned away, only to step back. "Did you notice," she went on, glancing around as if they might be heard, "that two pigeons had been taken this morning, one by the fountain, and one by the hedge?" She tipped up on her toes. "The duck hawk never takes two," she whispered.

Mr. Hansen winked again. "I saw that," he answered and grinned broadly.

"Isn't it lovely?" Miss Landry smiled and her blue eyes filled with lights. "I do hope he's careful." They both nodded, Miss Landry stepped back, and the truck moved slowly forward. She did not see Tako's tail hanging below the differential.

Tako was braced, unconsciously anticipating a morning of lakes and ice cream, when the truck suddenly made a sharp turn, bushes vanished, curbs came into view, and he realized he was out of the park and on strange territory.

The truck sped straight down Fifth Avenue. At red traffic lights Tako watched shoes and legs, wheels and exhaust. Then he was whisked into Washington Square Park. Here the truck stopped. Mr. Hansen got out and gathered his tools. He limped off to work. Tako remained where he was. He lowered his head and looked up Fifth Avenue. It was a canyon of misty verticals, so high that even he did not desire to explore their crests.

As the morning wore on he noticed the people were busy. They were gathering around squares of colors and lines, for the artists of Greenwich Village were hanging a show of their work. Just beyond the truck a bearded man in limp clothing began to hang a line of zigzag, eye-whirling pictures. Each time he put one up he stepped back and sat down on the truck fender. This went on for several hours. Eventually Tako's curiosity was aroused beyond caution and he dropped to the ground to see better.

People stared and talked, paintings swung in the breeze, but Tako was not interested in the avant-garde art. Much more fascinating was a squirrel that ran back and forth. He would take a nut from the hand of an artist, then sprint off to cache it somewhere in the park. On one occasion a peanut rolled against the truck's rear tire and the squirrel followed it. Tako thrust his head out.

"Well, hello there," the artist on the fender said. He slid to the ground, leaned over, and scratched Tako's head. Tako did not move. His success with men, he recalled, depended upon his doglike reaction.

"Whatcha think of the show?" the artist went on as his hand wound under Tako's chin and gave it a friendly squeeze. The coyote held still. A customer paused at a tennis shoe glued to a bed spring and framed in gold. The artist gave Tako a final pat and walked over to her. "What is it?" she asked.

"It's called 'The Masses,' " the artist answered. She walked on.

Sensing this was no place for him, Tako crawled

back to his hideout and lay down. The artist returned and circled the truck. "Come on, yellow
eyes," he called pleasantly, "where did you go?"
Tako did not budge from the differential.

It was mid-afternoon before Mr. Hansen returned to the truck and drove back to Central Park.
He pulled up beside the tool house and turned off
the engine. Tako was hot and thirsty. He dropped
to the ground just as the gardener stepped out of
the cab. They exchanged startled glances, then Mr.
Hansen blew him a kiss. Tako twisted his ears to
understand, felt pleasure, and darted into the
woods.

Several nights later he hunted a new area—the
walks and bushes around the Model Boat House. It
held no game, but ice cream sticks, still sweet with
flavor, were scattered about. He trotted from one to
the other, until he came to the water's edge where
a small lost ship was sailing. Tako cocked his head
sidewards as the wind filled its sails and drove it
toward him. To Tako most things that moved were
alive. He watched suspiciously, trying to pick up its
scent to ascertain what kind of animal it was. Suddenly it tacked on its own and started the other
way. The coyote pawed the water in curiosity,
found it shallow and waded in. The ship tacked

again and sailed in another direction. Tako rushed after it, discovered that it was inanimate but nevertheless interesting. He leaped upon it. The ship tilted, the sails crumbled, and the boat went over on its side.

It lay still like a dead mouse, and Tako was no longer interested. He climbed ashore on the north side of the pond and, suddenly lowering his nose to the ground, tracked a scent up the walk, around a playground, and down to 69th Street. He had found Poovey's trail, and there was something new in her scent. It was inviting.

At eleven o'clock the next night he was back at the 69th Street entrance waiting for Poovey. Rain was falling and the walk glistened in round whorls under each street lamp. Tako did not particularly want to wait in the rain. He saw a bench on which a newspaper lay and crawled under both. Here he groomed his fur until each hair stood separate and clean, then he washed his paws and pads.

Poovey entered the park at a bounce. Her master, Tako could see, was tall and thin. Frederick Wortman had dark hair and blue eyes, and he crackled as he moved in his fine black raincoat. His nose was narrow and large in his face. His manner was crisp. A senior in one of the city's private high schools, Frederick was a young man of manners and means, and his registered shepherd was his consuming after-school interest. Frederick Wortman, destined to inherit a chain of national hardware stores, was already rebelling at the idea of being a businessman. He found dog and horse shows, breeders and trainers much more to his liking than the society that frequented his parents' salon. The young man walked confidently a few yards into the park, unsnapped Poovey's leash, and let her run. She cavorted. Her man-combed hair smelled of pine oil. Frederick Wortman shouted an order.

Poovey ran to him, held her head high, then walked at his heels. Tako did not move. He only watched.

Suddenly Poovey found Tako's trail, swung back to the bench, then skittered to Frederick Wortman's heels. She had not growled or threatened. She had not left a message of possession or dominance. Tako did not quite understand. He put his nose on his paws while the two walked off into the park, and he was still in this position when they returned. He did not move as they passed and strode out of the park.

When they were gone, however, he dashed into the rain, rounded the Metropolitan Museum at a lope, and galloped back to the Fifth Avenue wall. He felt lively and restless. Scampering now along the protective wall of the park, he raced to 109th Street, leaped over, crossed Fifth Avenue.

He hurried past number 35 without pausing to check on Tenny. He wanted to be sure of his pigeons on the roof. Something about Poovey had inspired a need to check on his food supplies and hunt out new ones.

He climbed the stone steps, stood on the urn, and leaped to the fire escape. He ran up softly to the roof. The odor of pigeons grew sweeter as he climbed.

Suddenly he felt fear. He did not know why. But he instinctively crouched on his belly as a familiar odor, connected with a bad experience, terrified him. The smell was of metal and meat—the scent of the live trap in the desert. His nose located the danger, his eyes followed his nose. A trap lay near the bird cage. Stealthily Tako crept toward it as fear was replaced by anger. He grabbed the wire in his teeth and shook the trap until it clanged. The treadle snapped, the door slammed closed. Tako had rendered the trap ineffectual. He dropped it and stared, panting hard to relieve his fear. Then he went to the rear of the cage. The hole had been wired shut, but with paws and teeth he easily re-opened it and wedged in. Swiftly he took a pigeon, slid out of the cage, and trotted toward the fire escape.

A wind blowing over the edge of the building carried the scent of Rancid, the cat. Tako dropped his food, crouched, and waited. As the cat appeared on the top of the parapet, Tako leaped. Rancid spun backward meowing and hissing, then fell to the landing below. He yowled and howled. The window opened and Herb grabbed him. "Gotcha!" he cried, but he was no match for Mrs. La Gloria's tom. The cat spit, swung himself like a pendulum, and sank his claws into the man's arm.

Herb let go. Rancid leaped to the stairs and shot down them as the man cursed and thundered.

Tako heard Herb coming up the stairway to the roof. He picked up his pigeon and leaped over the wall to the fire escape as the door opened and Herb snarled out. "It's sprung!" he shouted when he saw the trap. "It's sprung."

While sounds of anger floated down from the roof, Tako reached the bottom landing and took stock of the street. People were passing below. He could not go down. Glancing around, he saw a window box of tall geraniums and crawled into it. Suddenly the door below opened and Herb roared out. He swung an umbrella aggressively as he scanned the sidewalk for Mrs. La Gloria's cat. Tako watched while he ate his pigeon.

An hour later he stood up, stretched, and took a vaulting leap to the fire escape on the next building. He leaped to the next, then shook his fur until it was loose, jumped to the ground, and trotted toward the river. As he approached First Avenue, he felt fear again. Another deeply imprinted scent warned him. He was at Joe's Auto Repair. Heeding the prickling rush of fright he bolted between a trash can and a gas pump, then peered out. Only the rats moved and shuffled. He took a step, but fear spiked his blood again. He pulled back, then a faint scent brought an image of Mr. Evans, the man who had frightened Tenny. Mr. Evans had been at Joe's Auto Repair recently. His aroma was on cement and air.

Tako waited. Mr. Evans did not appear. Cautiously he came forward and sought the man's warmest scent. It wound over and around the cars, then went to the sidewalk. It crossed the street and continued up 109th Street. Tako tracked hard, losing it now and then among the scents of other people. Finally he trailed it across Madison Avenue and up the street to number 35. It was so strong on the steps that Tako bolted for the park, never knowing that Cardy Evans had spent the afternoon with Tenny.

He had come on business.

"Tenny," he had said when she had offered him a seat on the green couch in the living room, "this coyote business is very serious. What do you know about it?"

She did not answer. He went on. "Your dad *did* bring him in, you know. The other men on the ship confirmed it. But how he got out of the cage and how he got to 109th Street is still unknown. I believe he followed someone who lives here." Mr.

Evans paused and studied Tenny. "And that someone, I believe, still knows where he is."

Tenny folded her hands. Mr. Evans continued.

"Please help," he said. "I saw him behind you
August twenty-fourth. Mrs. La Gloria saw him that
evening, and today I found where he dens, or did
den. I found coyote fur on a car seat in Joe's Auto
Repair. A microscopic examination by a mammalogist has confirmed it." He stared at her quiet oval
face and the curled lashes that were now touching
her brown cheeks. She was concentrating on her
hands.

"But he doesn't seem to be there now," he went
on. "We've searched every possible hideout at that
end of the block, and we're moving this way. Do
you know where he is, Tenny? We've got to get rid
of him."

Tenny smoothed her skirt. The gentle deed of
her daydreams was real again. She could do something wonderful; she could save the city from pests
and plagues. But a more beautiful event kept her
from speaking; her father was getting four oil
drums for José and the Street Family. If he learned
it was she who had turned Tako loose, she feared,
in fact she knew, he wouldn't get them. He'd pun-
ish her. A hundred dollars meant a lot to him, and

the drums meant a lot to her. She thought they would be her entrance into the Street Family, and this she wanted with all her heart. Tenny felt pain inside, a hot yanking pain. The conflicts were too intense to bear. The beautiful deed pulled her to speak. The necessary young family pressed her to silence.

She stood up. "I can't help you."

Mr. Evans slapped his knees and arose. "I'm sorry," he said. "I'd hoped you would."

He paused at the door.

"Well, there's at least another rumor to check now. I'm going to see Maria. Mrs. La Gloria said her daughter heard a coyote in the park at the end of the Philharmonic concert."

"Maria writes plays," Tenny whispered. "She makes things up."

Poovey

As October cooled the air Tako dug into the earth under the laurel bush. It was difficult work, however, for the ground was rocky. He would gain a few feet only to hit a boulder and have to dig back and around it. But he persisted.

One night he was clawing along a rock when his foot struck loosely packed earth. The soil moved and slid slowly downward. Tako thrust his nose into the cavity and sniffed. There were faint scents of metal. Curious, he dug until he came to a buried Con Edison electric cable. He yanked it with his teeth to dislodge it but got nowhere. Lying on his side, he scratched furiously but the cable did not move. He paused and sensed. The soil was warm; in fact it was heated. A subway generator lay off to the west and the transformers warmed the ground. With coyote wisdom he selected a spot in the warmth for his den.

He patted its floor and ceiling, made a cup for his body, and rested. Absolutely comfortable and secure, Tako groomed himself, feeling a sturdy brand of new fur under his tongue. The cold had started the growth of his winter coat with its sharp guard hairs and dense underfur. Tako was becoming a handsome and mature coyote.

In his warm den he dozed until hunger aroused him and drove him out into the midnight life of Central Park. Pausing in his doorway, he surveyed his domain. The laurel had folded with the cold and the tree leaves were spinning to the ground. A squirrel shifted in its winter nest of dry leaves balled in the limbs of the oak.

Suddenly the tiger cat slunk around the tree and crept toward the Loch. She was hissing at her kittens. One of them, small and black, was close to her, nudging and meowing. The tiger suddenly biffed it. The kitten tumbled backward and crawled under a sycamore leaf where she shivered in lonely fear. Tako ignored the mother and the rejected young, for the night was crisp and the moon was whitening the trails.

He trotted to the Loch for a drink and took the bridle path south, smelling the tangy scent of acorns and the mustardy aroma of ragweed pollen. As he approached the foot entrance to the park above the Metropolitan Museum of Art, he found a message from Poovey. Her aggressiveness was entirely gone. It was replaced by an invitation. Tako accepted it and tracked her.

Weaving in and out of the trees he trailed her to the Egyptian Obelisk, the tall historical monument behind the museum that meant no more to the coyote than a rock in the desert. He circled the object to see what lived around it. Scents told him the base was used primarily by squirrels to crack nuts on, and the top by the duck hawk to observe the squirrels. Insects had banged against it, fallen to the earth, and been devoured by a shrew that denned in a crack at its base. Tako steered away from the shrew. It smelled musty, and he knew from experience it was vicious. Satisfied that the Obelisk was a potential food source, Tako bounded southward on Poovey's scent again.

He stopped at the edge of the Model Boat House

where she had left an irritated-at-her-master note. It lay beside a popped balloon that had fallen into a cupcake wrapper. The wrapper was acrid with the scent of ants that had hauled away crumbs until the cold had sent them underground.

Suddenly Tako dropped to his belly. Poovey and her master were on the far side of the pond, he whistling, she jaunting along obediently at his heels, each of her hairs reflecting light like slender mirrors.

Tako did not approach for fear of the young man but, keeping to the bushes, he shadowed them down the woodland trail to the Children's Zoo.

Poovey knew he was following, but she never lost step with her master's stride, just threw up her head and pranced lightly as Tako wove in and out of the shadows. Once she glanced at him as he came darting back from a sprint and tossed her collar till it jingled. Frederick Wortman looked down irritably and barked a command. She walked quietly on.

At 69th Street she left the park, crossed the street, and disappeared into 870 Fifth Avenue. Tako waited a moment, then ran back through the woods sniffing, listening, and exploring the autumn night. He crossed the Mall to the café. The tasty

smells had disappeared, the crumbs and droppings were cleaned away, the tables and umbrellas gone. The café was closed for the winter. Tako went over to the Lake. Ducks slept far out on its waters, their heads in their back feathers as they rafted safely out of reach. Four great white swans slept on the shore. They awoke and hissed as Tako walked up to them. A drake with opened beak coiled his neck to strike. Tako stepped back. He did not want to tangle with the powerful bird.

He trotted along the Lake's edge. A screech owl called from a tree. Presently it dropped on a mouse and flew into a white pine.

Tako circled the Lake, walked up the deserted steps of the Mall, and sat down at the top. He looked over his kingdom, then stood up proudly and marched right down the center of the Mall, swinging his fur elegantly.

Crossing under a bridge around one o'clock, he arrived at the carousel. It was silent, its splendid painted horses still. The scent of popcorn and soggy ends of ice cream cones lured him onto its round platform, then in and out of the smiling horses. He sniffed the greasy motor that propelled the great merry-go-round and investigated the calliope. It made no sound, and so he did not realize that at last he had found the musician that had sung to him each summer morning.

Finishing off the popcorn and candy, Tako lifted his nose to trace another sweet odor. It was on a painted horse. Jumping onto its back he found a wad of chewing gum stuck on the arched neck. It smelled of very young fingers and peppermint. Tako bit it, turning his head from right to left until he tore it loose. Lightly, without sound, he dropped to the floor of the merry-go-round and trotted off with the gum.

Under a hawthorn bush by the Sheep Meadow he stopped to wipe the gum with his paw; he could not dislodge it from his teeth to swallow it. He chewed and pawed, went on a few feet, then sat down and chewed again.

As he stepped into the bridle path that led straight north to his laurel den, he gave up trying to swallow the gum. He no longer minded that it chewed on and on, and so Tako the coyote returned to his den that night chewing peppermint gum.

Before he retired he glanced up contentedly at the city, lifted his head, and wailed to Poovey. Then he dove into the earth. He skidded to a halt. Kitten scent wafted out of his bedroom. He inched forward, one foot exploring softly, then the next.

As he slid to the Con Edison wire, he came upon the black kitten that had been rejected by her mother that very night. She was trembling. Annoyed, Tako growled. The kitten stood up and spat bravely. Skinny, her back arched in defense, the small wild house cat faced the coyote. He snapped. She coiled against the cable and Tako passed. With a final snarl he wound down the tunnel to his warm room.

His long tramp had made him sleepy and he forgot the kitten as he circled, lay down, and groomed

his fur. Head on his tail, he slept. The night grew colder but Tako did not notice. The warm subway transformer radiated heat like a mother coyote.

He was awakened about three in the morning by a clacking purr. With a start he focused all his senses on his retreat. Then he felt, curled against his paw, the rejected and lonely daughter of the tiger. The kitten was sleeping contentedly, purring the purr of a house cat that has found its comfort. Tako glanced at the small black body and put his nose down beside her. She purred on. He nuzzled her gently, for he had a growing need for company—his own kind preferably, but in the coyote-less city the small black kitten quenched his loneliness. Her head rolled gently against his muzzle. They slept.

The Trail
by the Carousel

The next night Tako went hunting to the north
of his den. He snatched a weakened pigeon sleeping in the shelter of a paper bag by an overflowing
trash can and carried it back to the laurel bush to
dine. Unable to consume it all, he nosed its remains
into the earth near the tunnel and scratched dirt
over it. Then he set out swiftly to wait at the 69th
Street entrance for Poovey. No sooner had Tako
departed than the black kitten came tentatively out
of the den. She found the remains of Tako's dinner
and set upon it voraciously. The kitten had not
eaten in three days.

The Trail by the Carousel

At 69th Street Tako stretched out under a barberry bush and groomed himself until every hair gleamed. He straightened his whiskers and sensed for the warm presence of Poovey in the clanking city. She entered the park head high and prancing, for she knew Tako was near the entrance. She had caught his odor on the air as she stepped up on the curb. With dash Poovey and Frederick Wortman opened their strides and started across the park. Tako romped along beside them, keeping out of sight of the young man by putting the crowns of hills, the rocks, and the bushes between them. On the Sheep Meadow Frederick leaned down and unlatched Poovey's leash. She shook, pranced, and darted across the grass, her gold and brown fur flying, her tail whipping the air. Suddenly she veered, leaped over a rock, and rolled down on the hiding Tako. She bit his toes and pawed his cheek briefly —quickly, for her freedom depended on a prompt return. Tako sat on his haunches and watched her tumble and romp. Then a sharp command from Frederick catapulted Poovey over the rocks and obediently back. Tako slipped to the top of the hill, lay down in a crevice between the rocks, and watched Frederick fasten Poovey's leash. He led her back through the woods to 69th Street. Tako followed, always out of sight like a fluttering shadow, for he was now completely skilled at seeing heads begin to turn and moving away before eyes focused. He was an elusive wind in the park. He watched Poovey depart, then rushed exuberantly down the path. Swinging around the museum, he went home by way of the formal garden to check his holdings. All was well there. Leisurely he trotted to his den and crawled in. The black kitten was sleeping in the middle of his room. Tako nosed her aside. She awoke, rolled playfully to her back, and put her paws in the air. Her claws were withdrawn, and the small warm pads were soft as they touched Tako's nose. He shoved her aside and lay down.

Tako met and followed Poovey every night for three weeks. He waited for her under the bush, played with her briefly on her break to freedom, and came home striding down the Mall. He returned each dawn to the formal garden, but saw only Miss Landry. Mr. Hansen was raking leaves in other parks.

One night he felt a new intensity in Poovey even before she stepped into the park. Inspired, he rushed her. Frederick saw him. He picked up a stone and shouted. Tako ran off as the boy's arm unrolled. While he was hurling, the well-trained, obedient shepherd lowered her head, slipped her collar, and with a bound vanished with Tako. Frederick commanded and called; but she was off. The coyote was leading Poovey down the Ramble and north to the Great Lawn. They dug the earth as they turned and veered. In the field Tako chased Poovey in exuberant circles and Poovey chased Tako. Tako yipped and led her in graceful leaps through the Shakespeare Garden, over benches and trash cans to the rocks above the Lake. She followed lightly, her breathing coming faster with her excitement. She pranced. Tako pranced. They waded into the shallow water and chased the flock of ducks across the surface. The birds' wings made stinging wind sounds as they beat the water. Tako turned and nipped the lively shepherd. She galloped across a bridge, loped down a trail, and raced over another bridge. They came to the boat house. A woman with two poodles was jerked into the parking lot as her leashed males caught the scent of the shepherd and darted off to meet her. Tako slashed down on them, snarling dominantly. He shouldered one poodle into submission, bit the other to quell his interest in Poovey, and slipped into the darkness.

The woman shouted as the dogs wound her up in their leashes in an effort to escape Tako. When they could wind no farther they stopped and looked up at her, panting and wagging their tails.

Tako and Poovey ran down to the Lake, bounded over the tied-up row boats, and crossed the foot bridge to the Mall. They ran up the middle of the steps and headlong down the maple-lined boulevard. Two loving walkers saw them pass, exchanged smiles, and stepped closer together.

Over the lawns and through the woods the spirited animals romped until they came to the carousel. Tako jumped on the platform and waited for Poovey. When she leaped aboard he led her in and out of the legs of the painted ponies. Then he jumped up on one. He barked at Poovey, she jumped beside him, and, lightly, horse by horse, they circled the glorious merry-go-round. Suddenly Poovey stopped playing. She tossed her head and wagged her tail at Tako. Suddenly she sprang to the ground.

Tako leaped. His feet struck earth as quietly as dust. Poovey accepted the wild coyote.

Commands volleyed across the woods and lakes for an hour as Frederick called Poovey home. Eventually he ceased to call.

Several hours later Tako licked the shepherd's nose. His wariness returned. He listened and sensed danger. The clop of a horse's hoofs sounded on a distant wooden bridge. He slid into the bush cover and trotted north. Poovey followed him to the western bridle path and then whined and dashed away. Briefly she hesitated, sniffed the wind from the coyote, and took the bridle path toward the east. She went slowly up the steps, down the Mall, and around the Model Boat House. To her left she heard the horse neigh and the

voices of Frederick Wortman and the mounted policeman. She groomed her fur, then calmly walked
to meet them. Poovey wagged her tail, lowered her
head, and waited for her collar.

"Gosh, Andy," Frederick said to the policeman.
"She's never done this before."

"Is she in oestrus, Frederick?"

"Oestrus?"

"Does she want to have pups? Are the males following her?"

"They do on Fifth Avenue, but not in the park.

129

They stay away, so I thought she wasn't ready to breed."

"Does any one male protect her in the park? Could be there's a dominant dog that keeps the others off."

"I've never seen one." He thought a minute. "Except tonight . . . I saw a slinking animal at the Sixty-ninth Street entrance. I ran him off, however."

"Well, she's probably all right. There're no unleashed dogs here tonight."

"I hope not," Frederick said. "She's got good papers and I have a show dog all lined up for her."

"By the way, how long was she gone?"

"Musta been three hours."

"That's enough time. But I still think she's safe. I didn't see a dog anywhere." Frederick turned away. The policeman patted his horse and looked down on the young man. "Have you ever seen a tawny, yellow-eyed dog around here?"

"No," replied Frederick. "Why?"

"A friend of mine who's with the Health Service is lookin' for a coyote. He's got a hunch one came into the city last August on a freighter." Frederick gasped. The policeman smiled. "Don't worry," he said. "He's blocks uptown, we think.

Somethin's been raising a kind of hell on 109th Street. Killing a fellow's racing pigeons—big as a durn coyote, but I think it's a cat—a yellow tomcat named Rancid." He chuckled, and held the horse a moment longer while he studied Poovey. "Well," he finally said, "she's had a good run; that's all. She's too calm for a bitch who's mated."

"I sure hope she hasn't," Frederick said. "And particularly not to a coyote—gee, wild puppies —gee."

"Don't worry." He kicked his horse gently. "Good night," he called.

"Good night."

Frederick stared at Poovey who glanced up at him with soft eyes. "Good night!" he exclaimed to her.

Winter
in Central Park

One night Tako was hunting field mice by the carousel when a sudden wind crashed across the park bringing Arctic cold. He started home, head down to protect his eyes from the leaves and dust blowing in splinters across the roads and walks.

As he arrived at his den he was aware of stirrings in the leaves, of feet moving in the dark. He drew back. In packs and tribes the rats were moving. They were deserting their summer dens in the park and running toward the avenues and warm buildings. Screeching and screaming, nervous to be with each other, terrified not to be, the rodents of the underworld of the city launched hysterically upon their autumn migration. Tako snarled as they passed, slashing at him, their noses quivering, their eyes beady.

They swarmed under the oak tree where the tiger lived. She was on the limb, stalking like a cougar. A young one passed, she dropped upon it, wrestled it to death, and scratched up the tree again, her fur battered from the struggle. Tako leaped over a stream of bodies and dove for his den. The black kitten was crouched in the shadow of the entrance, stalking the moving herd. Tako wanted only to get out of their way. He slipped past her, rounded the rock, and came down on three fighting rats by the Con Edison cable. He ran them out with angry snaps, then hurried to the warm room.

Waiting for him was an enormous brown rat, one of the two species in the city—the brown came from Europe, the black from India. The two were bitter enemies. The rat leaped at Tako's throat and hung on viciously. Tako lashed his body and hurled the rat against the wall. It fell, got up, and leaped to Tako's back, cutting him with its chisel-like teeth. Tako rolled on it. The rat held. With a twist the coyote grabbed the beast, pulled, and shook.

The scent of blood brought four more rats down
the tunnel. Tako attacked them. They fought, but
it was more a battle of madness than defense. One
bit the air, another fought the wall, a third hurled
himself at Tako. The coyote began to back out of
the tunnel. Two more rats entered, screaming
wildly. Tako fought his way to the cable. He had
not survived this long in New York City to be done
in by rats. He slashed his way to the entrance.
Suddenly a rat ran under him to hide. It happened
to be a large black rat. Tako picked it up in his
mouth, turned, and dropped it into the tunnel
among the brown rats. Instantly they tore into it.

The battle changed. Rat fought rat in screaming fury. By the time Tako stepped into the night the snarling group were exiting with him, so terrified that they had no judgment. They wheeled and ran back. Tako swept into the woods. The rats ran in and out of his den, running, running with no sense —then some sped to the woods, some to the Loch where they were drowned, others went on toward the city.

For the rest of the night Tako lay near his den guarding it in the open where he could maneuver and battle the rats. As dawn came the migration slowed down. By the time the sun rose only one or two passed. Then none moved at all. The park was serene. The leaves lay still, the twigs did not stir. It was as if nothing had happened in the night.

Tako did not move either. He was too tired to get up. The sounds of the city came up—the buzz of people queuing up for buses, the rumble of the subway, the chorus of horns, the bleat of the whirlybirds. But Tako did not hear them. He slept.

Suddenly he was jolted out of his slumber. Something had moved. Rat-imprinted, he snarled and coiled to spring. He looked and relaxed. The black kitten crept out of a wind-stacked pile of oak leaves. She came over to him and rubbed her head against his neck. Her stomach was round and extended with good food. She passed Tako softly and walked down the tunnel into the city-warmed earth. Tako followed her, listening to the peregrin falcon call from the sky. The bird's wings whistled as she struck a tired and careless rat hobbling toward the warmth of the city.

The cold stayed for two weeks. Food became scarce as the sparrows and rats sought the building ledges and cellars to get out of the wind. The pigeons were not as active; they were conserving their energy.

One night Tako sped down the bridle path to the Lake. Jogging over the foot bridges, he came upon a message from Poovey. It was hostile again, but not aggressive. He tracked her to the park exit and sat down. She did not return.

Feeling lonely, he took his favorite trot down the Mall, crossed the transverse road on the stone wall, and came to the chess and checker house. No animals or birds stirred. The squirrels that were plentiful by day were balled in their winter leaf-nests high in the trees and the mice had burrowed below the frost line. The swans had been captured and brought into the Central Park zoo.

Tako usually stayed away from the zoo, although

once he had sat on the high rocks and watched the grizzly bear bathe. He went no closer for he knew better than to attract the attention of the animals. They would sense he was different from the city dogs. However, tonight most of the animals were indoors, sheltered against the bitter November weather, and Tako felt the need to explore. He walked down the hill, past the bear cage, through an arch, and onto the restaurant patio. He smelled food in a trash can, turned it over, ate some bread crusts, and trotted past the camel and zebra cages. The animals were not out.

Suddenly the splash of water startled him. He crouched to sense the night, saw neither man nor dog, and curiously moved to the edge of a pool. The water rippled, parted, and a sniffing face appeared close to his own. A sea lion greeted him. Tako turned his ears forward. The mammal rose out of the water until his head and neck were visible, then he rolled over like a wave and sank beneath the surface. In a few seconds he was back. Tako sat down and watched the performance. Suddenly the sea lion barked at him. The bark carried a note of warning and Tako slipped away as the night watchman came by on his rounds.

Tako went toward Fifth Avenue and searched the

trash baskets at the Pony Track. Smelling ice cream near the top of a basket, he jumped into the papers, picked up a half-eaten bar, and leaped out. He ate it in the playground by the seesaw. When he had finished he leaped onto the wall and traveled swiftly northward. However near 69th Street the many cars and the pedestrians became a threat. He padded his way into the woods, over the road, and, taking the sheltered edges of the walks, returned to his laurel den.

Food was hard to come by. Still hungry, he slipped into his tunnel. As he came into the dark room his nose gave him added sight. The black kitten was sleeping in the small cup she had scratched for herself. Beside her lay an unfinished bird. Its feathers were gray and singularly even. It was sweet and tender. Tako finished it eagerly, not knowing that the bird he had devoured was a record for New York. It was a Townsend Solitaire from the Rocky Mountains. The bird had been blown east on the storm that had held New York at 12 degrees, had run the rats into the old buildings, and had locked Tako's food supply into tree dens and deep tunnels. The small lost bird, a stranger to the city, gave strength to another stranger to the city. Tako's fight for survival went on.

The Odor of Pressure

One morning, having gone foodless for three days, Tako lingered in the formal garden. He stayed in the yew hedge, for the leaves had fallen from the roses, and he needed better cover. Not fifteen feet away a man sat with a morning paper. A bird hopped near. Tako struck.

Miss Landry, who was just arriving, saw the coyote spring and snatch the bird. She gasped in fright, not because he had taken a sparrow—she understood that—but because the man was present.

She turned to him wondering what to do; then, as Tako glided into the yew, Miss Landry sat down beside the man. Next she did an unheard-of thing for her—she talked to him. He studied her face and hat with such interest that he did not see the slinking animal. Such was her devotion to the coyote of Manhattan. When the wild beast was safe, she got up and walked briskly away. She was glad her poor departed mother would never have to know she had spoken to a strange man. As she passed the yew hedge she felt a delight in her desperate chicanery.

The next day the Arctic cold released New York and the air warmed above freezing.

The thaw was welcome to man and beast. It came about ten in the morning on December 15th. Tako and the black kitten felt its ease and crawled to their entrance. The squirrels were on the ground again and a few mice were venturing out of drain pipes and ground dens to gather grass seeds in broad daylight. Tako and the black kitten went to the deserted ball lot. He waited near a rock while the black kitten stalked a mouse. The mouse suddenly fled toward the coyote and he pounced upon it. Then he chased one to her. She killed it adroitly with her accurate paw-strike. In this coyote manner they hunted for several hours. The kitten sensed the virtue of a team and stayed with her large companion for several days.

Then the cold returned, the animals disappeared, and the black kitten took to the trees where she could stalk sparrows and reach into hollows for mice and woodpeckers. Tako could not join her. He cased the trash cans and lunch bags abandoned on benches at the Pond.

One night the black kitten brought a catbird back to the den. She laid it down. The bird had been left behind in the migration and had been living in the bushes along Harlem Meer. The first cold had weakened it, and the second freeze had made it an easy prey for the kitten. Tako devoured it.

The Odor of Pressure

The next night she brought home a robin, then a red poll, a bird of the north that had been driven south by the severe weather. The black kitten fared well on lost birds and, in the manner of cats, brought them to the den. Tako survived on the skills of the kitten and her deep instinct to lay food at the doorstep. The black kitten had another source of food, the Obelisk. Many birds struck it in the stormy weather and she picked them up and brought them home. With her help Tako lived well through the subzero weather.

His hunger satisfied, Tako felt another drive—to be with his mate. His instincts were to travel with her and to share the rearing of the pups. However, he was deprived of this, and could only wander to the 69th Street entrance and pace the bushes; but Poovey never came.

On December 19th the air warmed and Tako took off early to search for Poovey and make the rounds of his property. He paused by the Meer. The lights from the city were different, more numerous. On 110th Street small Christmas bulbs sparkled in windows, they glowed on street posts and around doorways. Tako did not wonder about them, he accepted them as he accepted the blooming and fading of the flowers and trees. Change was the way of the earth.

He jogged to 109th Street. He would try to enter this part of his territory again, despite the warnings of Cardy Evans, for tonight he was hungry and the pigeons were easy to catch. He crossed Fifth Avenue to number 35, curled low behind the trash cans, and judged the night.

A familiar footstep rounded the corner of Fifth Avenue and hurried across the street. He listened. It was Frederick Wortman. Tako crouched. The young man walked up the steps of number 35 and rang a bell. In a few minutes Tenny appeared.

I'm Frederick Wortman," he said. "I would like to speak to you about . . . well, a rather strange event."

"Yes?" said Tenny, glancing briefly at his expensive clothes and general elegance.

"I have a very valuable shepherd dog," he began. "Poovey, I call her. It seems she was bred about a month ago when she broke away in Central Park." Tenny shifted feet. Frederick went on.

"The policeman who was with me that night dropped by the other day to say that 109th Street was buzzing with rumors of a coyote. A woman who runs a grocery store told him you might know something about it.

"I just need to know for sure if there really is a coyote, because if there is, he's probably the father

of the pups my dog is pregnant with. And if he is, you see, I'll have to have them aborted immediately."

Tenny watched the young man's anguished face and listened thoughtfully, but did not speak.

"Do you know anything about him?" Frederick persisted. "I *must* know."

Tenny hesitated. The idea of an abortion horrified her. She realized she might be able to prevent it.

"Where do you live?" she asked carefully.

"On Fifth Avenue and Seventy-sixth Street."

Tenny quickly caculated. "Thirty-nine blocks away." She sighed and stepped out of the doorway, looked both ways, then whispered, "Yes, there is a coyote in Central Park; but he is not the father of your dog's puppies."

Tako sensed a new emotion in Tenny's voice. The gentle hurt that had once softened her voice was replaced by a confident dominance. He could not know that the Street Family had asked her to join them.

"He must be," Frederick said dispiritedly.

"He can't be. He lives at my end of the park. Do you know anything about animal territory?"

"Yes, of course."

"Then you know they stay in a very specific area, all their lives."

"Yes, I know that; but I don't know what a coyote's home range is."

"Well, I've looked it up. It's no more than two hundred acres, usually less. Tako's two hundred acres include from here to the river, and a small end of the park."

"Are you sure?"

"Yes."

Frederick Wortman's shoulders drooped slightly as he relaxed. Then his brow wrinkled and he turned back to Tenny.

"Maybe you're right. Do you know where he dens? A den kind of helps locate his range."

Tenny leaned back against the rail. "I don't know if I can trust you."

"What do you mean?"

"Certain people want to find the coyote . . . and kill him. Knowing where he dens would make it easier. If I tell you, you must never tell anyone . . . no one, no one at all."

"You have my word." Frederick straightened tall. His face was so sincere that Tenny felt her secret would be kept in his confidence.

"It's way up at the northwest corner of the park,

deep in a stand of trees. It's beyond Harlem Meer and not quite to the fort. I found it one day when I took a short cut home. Mr. Wortman"—Tenny looked sympathetically into his face—"Tako *can't* be the father. You see, you live too far away."

Frederick nodded slowly as he recalled the night that Poovey had been bred. "I was way below the Metropolitan Museum when she got away. She didn't go far, 'cause we found her again almost where I lost her."

His face brightened. "This is great news!" Frederick reached out and took Tenny's hands in both of his. He squeezed them happily.

"As far as I'm concerned," he said, "there is neither a coyote nor a den." He spun on his toe, dashed down the steps, and, leaping over the gutter, ran across the street and around the corner.

Tenny stood still. She smiled happily as the glow of the gentle deed came over her. She had finally done it. She had helped someone, and, even nicer, an animal, too.

Tako did not move. The environment was not right. Mr. Wortman was off his territory. Tenny was different. He waited.

Three hours later most of the lights went out in the buildings, and the people deserted the streets.

The Odor of Pressure

Tako drifted swiftly down the sidewalk to the pigeon house, went up the fire escape and over the parapet. The live trap was set again. He sprung it, wedged into the cage, and took a pigeon. He knew better than to eat it at this dangerous site. He leaped over the wall onto the next roof and devoured it behind the water tower.

Tako was uneasy. He was alarmed by Tenny's new mood and the presence of Frederick. He searched for a new and circuitous route home. This the roof tops offered. Running and leaping, he moved along the top of the city. He passed chimneys and TV antennae, clothes-line poles and deck chairs—but no people. He came to the last building on the block, felt the warmth of a chimney, and lay down beside it. He slept through the dawn and the next day.

That night he took one more pigeon, sprung the live trap again, traveled the roofs to Lexington Avenue, and wound down the fire escape to the ground. He started back to the park.

The scents at number 35 were fear-provoking. Leon was home and Mr. Evans had been in and out. Tako paused. Then he lifted his head. A hammering followed by a bell-like tone sounded down the street. Presently a deeper note vibrated. This was followed by a ripple of clear music. The drums were being made. Tako crossed the street.

The door to number 35 opened. The once friendly spot had become a fear-filled trigger. Tako bolted for shelter. There was no place to hide but the low, gaping mouth of the storm sewer. He wedged himself in, dropped to a ledge, and looked down into the basement of the city. Cold drafts came up from the darkness and, as his eyes adjusted, he saw a great tunnel lined with bricks and glistening with water. It plunged toward the river.

Tako lay down on the ledge as Mrs. La Gloria stepped out of number 35. "Now, Tenny," she said "you gotta help. You gotta tell us where he is. Herb Schwartz is gonna kill my cat if he don't find out who's taking his pigeons. I figger the coyote's doin' it, and I mean to find him. Lots of people heard him at that concert—'cept you—and Elaine and Maria, but they're just stickin' up for you, now that you're a member of that crazy group. But you won't talk, and let me tell you, you ain't helpin' no one."

"I'm sorry," said Tenny.

"Humph," snorted Mrs. La Gloria.

When she departed Tako slipped out of the storm sewer, flashed across Fifth Avenue, and sauntered back to the warm room and the black kitten. He dozed restlessly, sensing the pressures of a strange hunt.

Three days before Christmas it snowed. Tako lay with his nose out of his den and watched the white flakes fall. They were quiet. They whitened the air as they fell around him. Curious, he tasted them. They disappeared and water slid down his throat.

The black kitten stepped over his head, sniffed the whiteness, and started off into the woods. She flipped her feet as she walked. Tako followed her for a few yards, stopping now and then to look down and understand the new environment. Once he pounced to defeat it, found it soft and airy, and changed his mood to play. He frolicked through the woods, rolling and tumbling. Finally the snow blew too hard and he skittered home over the frozen Harlem Meer. The kitten was already sleeping.

The storm blew itself out on Christmas Eve and Tako took out across the park to see what changes it had created. He went south, listening to the peal of bells and the merry vocal notes of the many people who were up and moving on this night.

Tako passed the Reservoir, heard ribald laughter from the windows of the 22nd Precinct Police Sta-

tion along the transverse road, and finally reached
the alder bushes at 69th Street. Absolutely no messages had been dropped by Poovey, and yet his instinctive sense of timing told him his pups would
be born soon. He got up, circled in confusion, and
followed the wall back to the formal garden. He
dug back the snow in the yew hedge and crouched,
listening to bells and Christmas carols that rolled
out with electrical voices.

Wild Puppies

As the sun rose on Christmas morning Tako was too sleepy to lift his head even at the vibrations from Miss Landry's feet. He did twitch his ears, however, when Mr. Hansen spoke, for it had been a long time since he had seen or heard the gardener.

"Merry Christmas, Miss Landry," he said.

"Merry Christmas to you. It's a pleasure to see you. I thought you were in the greenhouses all winter." She threw her bread on the snow. Tako heard the crackle of birds' wings and smelled their dusty bodies.

"My family's all grown," he said, "so I take the duty for the young men with children on Christmas."

Miss Landry glanced around. The park was empty. "I'm glad you're here," she said and stepped closer to him. "Ever since the storm, there has been a man from the U.S. Public Health Service around as well as a mammalogist from Albany."

"Oh? What do they want?"

"What do you think?"

Mr. Hansen studied her face. "Our coyote?"

"Our coyote," she said. "They questioned me one day, then asked me to cooperate by looking for slender doglike footsteps in the snow."

"Well, now," Mr. Hansen said. "What do they want?"

"They want to kill him."

"Kill him?"

"Yes. They say he's a danger to the public health."

"Mmm." Mr. Hansen rubbed his chin.

Miss Landry went on. "I didn't tell *them,* but I look at it this way. If birds and mice and coyotes are in the Park, they're here for a reason. They have as much right as we do."

"They surely do," said Mr. Hansen pulling his

coat collar tighter. "How are they going to get him?"

"They're waiting for a new snow. Then they'll track him to his den and trap him."

Mr. Hansen crossed the walk. He looked into the crab apple tree garden. "I used to see him around here," he said.

"Well, if he's here I'm going to help him," she said, adjusting her boots, and stepping into the undergrowth. "Look!" She pointed to footprints in the snow. "Coyote?"

"Could be," Mr. Hansen answered, and leaned down to have a closer look.

"Well, then, I have a little duty." She swished a whisk broom from her pocket and swept away the tracks. Mr. Hansen smiled. He moved on, found some more, and Miss Landry whisked those away, too.

"Isn't it thrilling that he's here," she said finally.

"Yes," Mr. Hansen replied. "Yes, indeed."

"Can we meet after every snow and swish, Mr. Hansen?" she asked shyly. "It's so wonderful to know a wild animal is with us."

Mr. Hansen smiled and rubbed his hands together. "I just like to drift off to sleep at night thinking about it," he confessed. "He's a champ, Miss Landry. I'll do all I can to help him."

They walked the gardens for a long time before they were satisfied with their work. Then Miss Landry put away her broom, folded her paper bag, and went up the steps to Fifth Avenue.

"Have a happy day," she called.

Mr. Hansen grinned pleasantly. "I will. I like secrets," he called.

The pressure of the hunt increased. Two weeks later Tako returned to 109th Street. He leaped onto a hill of snow stacked in the gutter and surveyed his land. He was about to cross to number 35 when the scent of danger alerted him—steel and meat. The old fear of the trap in the desert sped through him. He moved cautiously now, following the scent to a cellar. He eased down the steps and found the trap. He snatched it in his teeth, shook and sprung it, then smelled the hands that had put it there. He filed this odor carefully so that he would recognize the scent when he met it again. It was the odor of the mammalogist from Albany, Dr. James Lockspur.

As he registered the smell, down the street in the big red apartment building Dr. Lockspur was talking to Mr. Bedford, Elaine's father.

"Your daughter belongs to the Street Family, does she not?" he was saying as Tako nosed the trap once more.

"Yes," Mr. Bedford answered.

"A gang?"

Mr. Bedford sat up. "A gang?"

"A gang that has set a coyote loose on the city?"

Mr. Bedford laughed. "You read the papers too much," he said and ran his fingers through his red hair. "They're really a pretty simple lot. Like to be with each other, that's about all. They yak away about things they feel and do . . . oddly enough, like a family. They argue, criticize each other, stick up for each other, get mad—you know. Some act like dads and take care of others. Some act like mothers, protecting and soothing . . . some, I must confess, act like babies. But as for anything else, you've got the kids all wrong."

"Well, be that as it may," the mammalogist said crisply, "this coyote must be found. Several poodles and terriers have been infected with intestinal and lung parasites. The animal is a danger to the city."

"What do you want me to do?"

"Get the kids to pry the story out of Tenny. I think she knows where he dens. Mrs. La Gloria reported that Maria had hinted at this."

"I can't do that. Those kids aren't gonna tell me or any other adult. Tenny's one of them now. She's family, secret or no secret, danger or no danger. You work on 'em."

The mammalogist rose to go. "I don't understand the lack of cooperation around here," he said. "I find not only the Street Family impossible, but many of the people on this street are actually on the coyote's side. They refuse to let me set box traps in their cellar wells."

"You don't understand 109th Street," Mr. Bedford interjected. "We're a mixture from around the globe. We don't have much, but we do know how it feels to be pushed around and persecuted. We understand this animal. Matter of fact, I'm on the coyote's side, too." He laughed. "He ain't hurtin' anything but a lot of rich men's dogs, so far as I can see."

"It's my job to get him," Dr. Lockspur said. "And I will." He shook Mr. Bedford's hand.

Mr. Bedford reneged slightly. "I'll tell you what I'll do, I'll talk to Tenny, but I can't promise a thing. It's pretty exciting to be protecting a coyote against the authorities." He chuckled again.

"I guess I've been too long in too many ivory towers," the mammalogist said, with a glimmer of insight. "Good night." He slapped Mr. Bedford's shoulder and grinned.

A week later a light snow fell. Tako and the black kitten hunted the subway. They left no tracks for they came out as the snow was falling and their footsteps were covered.

However, after the next snowfall, they tramped to the baseball field. Tako led the way, the black kitten followed in his footprints, and her small stride and belly-touching leaps blotted out Tako's big tracks. They wandered the entire field, one behind the other, but game was scarce and they circled home early, the kitten behind the coyote.

When Dr. Lockspur examined the ball field in the morning he paused over the tracks but they bore no resemblance to a coyote print.

After several unrewarding expeditions Dr. Lockspur picked up the telephone and called Cardy Evans.

"Cardy," he said, "I've covered the entire north end of the park. There just aren't any coyote tracks. I'm beginning to doubt if he's real. Maybe I better get on back to Albany."

"Stay," Mr. Evans said. "Five yellow-furred coyote pups—whadya call 'em—ki-dogs?—were born to Wortman's shepherd last night."

"You're kidding."

"Like to come down and see them?"

"Yes."

"Meet me at the Madison Avenue Animal Hospital," Cardy's metallic telephone voice said. "I'd like a verification."

The Father

The next morning a high-pressure area from the south brought warm air to New York. The snow melted and the starlings appeared in the meadows in the brighter colors that marked the beginning of their breeding season. The sparrows flew back to the park from the buildings and a few rats deserted the overcrowded basements to return to the land. Tako was lying in the alders by the 69th Street entrance watching the apartments on Fifth Avenue. Poovey did not appear.

Late in the morning he scratched a shallow den in the earth under the bushes. Once he whined, not quite understanding what was wrong with him, for there were no scents, no sounds or sights to inspire him, and yet, he was responding to a deep vague sense that his family was somewhere. That night he trotted back to the formal garden and inspected the wisteria arbor.

There he fulfilled an old coyote tradition. He was not hungry. He and the black kitten were finding more food in the park than they could use; and yet Tako killed a bird in the vines. He stood with it in his jowls for a minute, then dropped it. He was about to walk away but could not. He took it in his teeth again and, following a vague impulse, ran to the wall and all the way along it to 69th Street.

The Father

He arrived at the entrance, slipped under the alder bushes, and circled the shallow den he had made. There he laid the bird. It was for Poovey and the pups. Instinct and inherited behavior were governing him. Even Tako did not fully understand, for there were no pups to guide his actions. He nosed the limp bird and turned away.

He returned the next night and the next, and on each trip he left a rodent or a bird. And each time he shook his head, listened for the sounds he wanted to hear, heard them not; and wandered aimlessly toward the zoo. He walked among the animals, feeling comfort in their odors and scents.

On the third night he lay down by the sea lion's pool. The animal swam to him, sniffed, and rolled back into the water. When he emerged Tako ran to meet him. He snapped playfully. The sea lion snorted and rolled out of sight. After a while Tako anticipated where the sea lion would come up. He ran to a spot and waited. He was right. The sea lion blew water in the coyote's face in surprise. Tako cavorted to another spot. He met the sea lion again, for the water paths the animal took were a pattern. He repeated trails even as Tako did. They played quietly until the city began to stir, then Tako sauntered off to the empty Marionette Theatre. He wedged himself under the door and fell asleep among torn tickets and bright scenery.

As the days passed the birds piled up at the 69th Street entrance, and all this time Tako did not return to his laurel den. He hung around the zoo where the sea lion filled his need for the companionship of his family. His paternal instincts shifted to the funny water beast, then died.

One night he sat down in front of the bear cage. The great grizzly was moving in her den. Presently she caught his scent and shuffled over to him. She lay down against the bars and stared. Tako stared back. The bear reached through the cage but could not touch him so her paw hung limply over the iron bar. They stayed close to each other, Tako on the walk, the great bear on her cement pavilion, both napping until the unwiseness of his exposed position awoke Tako and he remembered his warm den. He started home.

He did not get beyond the Loch. The scent of the man who had set the trap on 109th Street reeked on the leaves. Tako tried another route home. He went back to the formal garden, turned north, and followed the wall to Lenox Avenue. The odor of the man was here, too. Tako sensed trouble.

At the west side of Harlem Meer he came upon another live trap. Dr. Lockspur's scent covered it. Tako lifted the trap over his head, heard the door slam shut, threw it down, and trotted to the garden. He dug himself a den under the English ivy, and stayed there for a day and a half, not even venturing forth when Miss Landry came to feed the birds. He felt surrounded. Aggressive people and scents filled 109th Street, and now they permeated the northern end of the park.

Tako could not know that Dr. Lockspur had verified that the pups had been sired by a coyote. That was all he needed to know to step up the hunt.

Just four days ago Frederick Wortman had stood in the sterile white whelping room of the animal hospital and looked down angrily at his dog and her litter. Dr. Lockspur was on one side of him and the gentle but conscientious Cardy Evans on the other. "Now what do we do?" Frederick Wortman asked. "You say the pups have fur, not hair like a dog's. You say this means coyote."

"We get rid of the pups," Dr. Lockspur answered curtly. "We can't let them go into homes. They're wild."

Frederick covered his face.

"That's right," Mr. Evans echoed and stuffed his hands in his pocket. As he glanced at the young man he thought back on his interrupted training to be a veterinarian, and his own painful conflict about whether to help man or beast. He had been

sent out by his professor to trap and kill, by injection, an infestation of house cats that were living wild near a suburban community. He had rounded up seven of them. Cardy had had no feelings about his duty until he was driving them back to the lab. Then one got out of the cage, came over the back of the seat, and curled quietly on his shoulders. It was all black with a white star on its face. It was shiny, clean, and well-muscled. A glance at it and he slowed the car down, opened the door, and turned the cat loose near a farmhouse. That evening in the lab the parasitologist clapped Cardy on the back and said, "Well done, Evans. Every cat in that batch was carrying a parasite transferrable to hogs and cattle."

Cardy couldn't sleep that night. He paced the floor in anguish. A sick cat was loose by a farmhouse where children lived. At three in the morning, he walked all the way back to the spot where he had released the cat. At nine o'clock in the morning he found it at last. Nevertheless, he still found it difficult to end the animal's life, and when it was over he sat with his head in his hands and argued with himself that man must come first.

He was feeling the same way now about the coyote, when Frederick suddenly knotted his fists and struck the air. "That little brat!" he blurted angrily. "She deceived me! That black crow deceived me. You can't trust a nigger!"

Mr. Evans looked at him in horror—gritted his teeth and stood still.

"Tenny! Tenny!" Frederick shouted. "That's her name. She knows where the den is."

Dr. Lockspur grabbed him. "How do you know?"

"She told me." His narrow nostrils flared. "But I feel no obligation to her any more. She deceived me. She told me he lived in the north end of the park. But he *did* breed Poovey! She deceived me!"

Mr. Evans didn't speak. He let Dr. Lockspur handle the boy. Sadly he walked to the whelping box and picked up a fat gold pup. It's nose was blunt with puppyhood, but more pointed than that of a domestic dog. It's tail was curled low. He rubbed it's head and placed it affectionately against his shoulder.

"Where is the den, Frederick?" Dr. Lockspur demanded sternly. "This is important."

Suddenly the young man blushed. He noticed the dark bowed head of Cardy Evans. He rushed to him, ignoring Dr. Lockspur. "I'm sorry, Mr. Evans," he blurted. "I didn't realize . . . you're not like most of them."

"You better hush," Cardy said calmly. "You're making it worse. It's okay."

"Where's the den, Frederick?" Dr. Lockspur repeated in measured tones.

Slowly Frederick faced him. "It's between the East and West Drives above the Loch," he said gravely. "That's all I know. She found it cutting home from school through the woods." He shrugged. Dr. Lockspur picked up his coat and hat.

"What about the pups?" Frederick asked pitifully.

"They'll be taken care of in the morning," the mammalogist answered. "I'll see to it."

"But Poovey?" His voice was weak. "She seems to like them. Will she mind?"

"She'll get over it." Dr. Lockspur said curtly and tapped Cardy Evans on the shoulder. "I think we can end this case. Let's go!"

Cardy Evans replaced the pup, stood wistfully looking at it for a moment, then turned. Frederick Wortman reached out a limp hand.

"I don't know why I said it," he whispered. "I'm really very liberal. Sorta came out—from nowhere."

"That's where it lies," Cardy said, and squeezed the thin arm. "Kinda scares you that it takes more than thinking right to take it away. Thanks for the information." He smiled.

The Posse

Tako came home the next night in a light snow-fall. It was now five days since the verified birth. He tossed his head and breathed the sharp crystals into his lungs. He had checked the paths and stream beds for the odor of the man with the traps and had found it so faint that he did not feel fear as keenly as he had the past night.

Before he entered the den, he listened. The city throbbed with the sounds of human living in which he had come to take comfort. He lowered his head and pressed down on his haunches to enter.

Out of the darkness charged the black kitten. She spat viciously at Tako and thrust her hairs erect on her sinewy body. Tako drew back in surprise, whipped his ears forward, and sat down. Something was wrong. He snarled at her, trying to dominate, but she persisted in spitting. He waited for her frenzy to pass, put his head down on his paws, and watched her. She paced before him, arching her back, then sauntered down the tunnel. Tako skidded forward on his belly. Knowing the pain of the cat, he moved carefully. Suddenly she rushed him again. She spat and struck. She walked sideways in defense. Tako did not understand.

Then from the depth of the tunnel came the tiny mews of new cat life. So that was it. She had kittens. Tako edged to the room on his belly, smelled the wet beasts, then pulled away as the mother once more hissed and spat. Backing out of the tunnel, he lay under the laurel judging what to do. He finally trotted off. The den belonged to the black kitten now. He knew better than to challenge a mother cat.

This was no loss to him, he had other retreats —the yew bush, the alders at 69th Street, the Marionette Theatre, the English ivy, the bandshell, the formal garden. He decided on the latter and the English ivy. He trotted off.

At dawn he was awakened by footsteps he thought were Miss Landry's. Then he tensed. The footsteps were not hers. They were the steps of two men: Mr. Evans and Dr. Lockspur. The mammalogist carried a pack.

"The kid took the Mount trail," said Mr. Evans, stepping out in front. "I asked José. Tenny had talked to him and he was quite cooperative. Said he'd convinced her we'd be gentle with the animal and that a plague really could get started."

"Good. About time."

Mr. Evans glanced back. "Nice kid, that José," he said warmly. "He's got that whole Street Family playing steel drums, you know."

"No, I didn't."

"They're good. Darn good. They've got one number called 'I'm Hiding My Way Out of Here.' It's terrific."

"Hmm. What's that mean? I don't get it."

"This way? Across the drive and through the woods?"

"Yes, north toward the fort."

Dr. Lockspur kept turning and checking. He was beginning to see Tako's world—the garden where birds gathered, the lake for water and probably thirsty rats, the trees . . . all good coyote country. He wondered why he had not seen it before. At the drive he noticed rat holes and the droppings of mice as belatedly he put his training into practice.

"This is terribly interesting, Cardy," he said. "It's so obvious. A coyote would naturally select this hill." He hurried when he saw the laurel. "I'll wager it's there," he said.

Cardy knew also when he saw the bush. He pushed back the leaves and looked into the round denway. He was pleased and, at the same time, sad.

"Now," he said to Dr. Lockspur, "what do you suggest?"

"Well, I've learned this much about the Street Family. We do this humanely. I've brought a den bomb. It's been designed by the Pest Control Bureau of the Fish and Wildlife Service for groundhogs and other vermin. It's quiet . . . kills them in the den.

"But"—and his face lighted at his own insight—"I won't do that. I've become a sociologist during this tour of duty. We can't kill this fellow here. We 'capture' him and take him to a far-away lab, preferably Albany, for a quiet death, maybe a month from now when all is forgotten. So I have a very light bomb. It'll drive him out. We net him." He pulled out a nylon net to demonstrate. "It won't be so brutal. I think that's important to the Street Family. Then we'll dispose of him quietly and that'll relieve the Health Service and people like Mrs. La Gloria."

"I'm tired," said Cardy. "I don't think you quite understand the kids. But if you don't even understand their songs, I can't explain it. Let's just get it over with."

Dr. Lockspur placed the bomb quickly, putting it just far enough into the den to get results, then lit the fuse. He threw one end of the net to Cardy, and held the other. They were ready.

Cardy Evans concentrated very hard, trying not to feel anything as the fuse burned down into the den. A muffled explosion shook the earth. They spread the net. Nothing happened. They waited. Even Cardy was puzzled as he leaned forward and stared into the smoke.

Another minute passed. A faint cry came from the ground.

The black kitten came out of the den. In her mouth a round kitten hung. She dropped it beside Cardy Evans and ran back into the smoke and gas.

"Oh, jeeez," said Dr. Lockspur, wiping his head. "A cat." Cardy Evans said nothing. He was watching the den. The black kitten brought him one

more curled body, then, purring and meowing, dropped dying against his knee. He touched it and looked away.

"I don't think I'm cut out for this job," Cardy said and slumped over his knees.

"People come first," declared Dr. Lockspur, but he, too, put his head down and sighed. "Where do we go from here? We can't get sentimental."

Cardy rallied and forced himself to think of the job.

"Just tell me more about coyotes," he said.

"I'm a book naturalist," Dr. Lockspur confessed. "I just don't know what's operating here."

"Well, thanks, because I don't either. What's a cat doing in a coyote den?"

Dr. Lockspur pounded his fist against a tree. "You know, Cardy," he said, "once a famous ecologist said to me, 'Man has gained intelligence but lost the greatest asset—instinct.' I never paid any attention to that because to me intelligence couldn't be beat. But right now I wish I had instinct. My intelligence isn't getting me anywhere."

Cardy took a deep breath. "Let's use basset hounds," he said. "They still have instinct."

"Yes, that's a good idea."

The Chase

Three days later Tako crawled onto the differential of the park truck to listen to the voice of a hound. The notes were sporadic. Tako twisted his ears. The tone became definite, the accents sharp. These sounds indicated the hound was working a trail. Furthermore, it was his. He sensed this by the tone of the hound's voice. Earlier it had been high and snappy—a squirrel or a rabbit. Then it had changed by the Meer and opened into a mellow bay.

Tako had heard this note before in the desert of his puppyhood. It said coyote as clearly as a running yap said "deer." Silence—the hound had lost the scent. When he picked it up again the note sounded confused. Tako had not been in the territory for several days, and the dog had only a few urine-posts to go on. These were far apart.

Tako put his head down. His territory was narrowing. The den area was unsafe, and most of 109th Street. Only the formal garden and the southern part of the park were unthreatened, but a live trap near the Metropolitan Museum had warned him to move south with caution. The hound stopped baying and Tako lay still.

The sun was high when he heard Miss Landry's footsteps. He revolved his ears and listened. It was late in the day for her to come to the park and he did not hear the familiar rattle of her paper bag. Her steps were hesitant and wary. Tako dropped his head to see. Miss Landry stood beside the crab apple tree garden, glancing this way and that as she leaned over and stuck something in the ivy. She straightened up, opening her handbag, took out a handkerchief, and wiped her fingers. Then she put on her gloves and departed at a swift click.

The garden was quiet. No people moved. Tako

twitched his nostrils, caught a rich odor, and dropped to the ground to follow the scent to the crab apple trees. Two large chunks of beef lay on the ivy leaves. He gulped them down, enjoying the refined flavor, then plunged back to the truck. The hound bayed by the Mount. Tako glanced in his direction as the voice changed, announcing not a coyote but a squirrel.

As he stood behind the truck Tako saw a narrow space in the rear between two stacks of empty flats. He leaped onto the carrier and wedged into the gap. Covering his nose to avoid the acrid smell of a bag of bone-meal fertilizer, he lay listening for the dog.

At noon he heard the hound working his way toward the formal garden. Tako lifted his head in concern. Then the motor of the truck started and Mr. Hansen drove to Fifth Avenue and sped downtown to Sheridan Square Park. The gardener got out and, with a sigh, went to work. Tako slept peacefully.

On their return, Mr. Hansen parked the truck behind the service building for the night and greeted several other gardeners. The rumor of the coyote was now a fact and the gardeners spent a few minutes jokingly planning escape routes for him. A Greek from 40th Street suggested that the whole tale of the coyote of Manhattan was just a continuous "happening" planned by the people of Greenwich Village to keep the park personnel out of Washington Square Park where they scolded the villagers for trampling the flowers. Delighted, an Armenian from Brooklyn agreed and suggested they turn a lion loose in Greenwich Village to see what kind of "happening" they would have. The men laughed, but they were proud of their coyote. The Greek took up a collection for dog food, saying, "We oughta feed him good so he can run good." Finally they broke up and wandered toward their subways and buses.

Tako heard them depart. He flicked his ears as the park visitors wandered home. Only the beat of the horse-drawn hansoms sounded from the roads. The park was settling down for the night. He jumped from the truck, crossed a bridge into the Shakespeare Garden, and urinated in the fountain. He wanted to leave no message for the hound. This garden was deserted, the plants bent down for the winter, the corners of the steps filled with wind-blown leaves. Tako raised his splendid head into the air. His fur blew back, his tail marked the wind direction. He felt comfortable for the first time in weeks.

The night was gusty. He lowered his shoulders

into the blows and started for the Great Lawn. In the open he could keep an eye on man and beast. Halfway across the yard he stopped and circled back. He wailed as he ran, following a faint and familiar scent across the field to the Obelisk—to the footpath under the East Drive—to the road wall.

Poovey! he was following Poovey. She was back. But her messages were not of pups and a rollicking home life, but of pine-scented bath soap—and, once more, dominance and hostility. He did not understand, for the coyote mates for life and, once mated, devotion lives from year to year. It was far beyond his comprehension to fathom the domestication of the dog and the breeding out of the canine behavior. He reached 69th Street running into the wind. A patrolman saw him swinging by, turned and watched. Tako ducked under a bench, ran north, then circled south to the alder bushes.

Poovey was not around. He waited through the windy night, occasionally wailing to the tall stone buildings. Before dawn he trotted back to the formal garden, found another offering from Miss Landry, and judged the hunt.

The hound gave voice, between the Metropolitan Museum and the garden, baying the note of "coyote." Tako tasted the wind, sensed the dog would soon close down on him, and headed for the bridle path.

He knew Central Park. Aware that mounted police passed every day he sought out the strong feces of their horses. He trotted right in them until his own scent was lost in the stronger scent of the horses. Then he headed south, splashed through a puddle of water in the winter-drained wading pool to lose his trail in the water, and slipped back to Mr. Hansen's truck. He attacked the bag of bone meal. He forced open the tough paper with teeth and claws and, as the fuming fertilizer spilled, he rolled his body in it. When he was satisfied that he had changed his scent he curled and lay loose to listen.

It took until sunup for the hound to follow the coyote trail to the pool and by the time the dog found it on the other side of the pool Mr. Hansen had driven off with the truck and Tako was dozing by the merry-go-round.

In pleasure he listened to the sparrows. They peeped and bickered. Presently a female alighted on the edge of the truck. She held a paper clip in her beak, chirping despite it. She carried it over Tako's head to an eave of the carousel and pushed it into her nest of string, ribbon, belt buckles, pennies, and bottle tops from the park. When she had placed the paper clip decoratively on the structure she came to the door of her scrabbly apartment and chirped brightly. The breeding season was just beginning. The sparrow was refurbishing her home. She did no more, however, for the urge to nest was weak. The bird spent the rest of the day at the sanctuary by the Pond stealing corn grains from the ducks.

Tako was driven back to the service building at dark.

The next day he did not hear the hound. The silence made him uneasy. He did not know what to expect, so he stayed in the back of the truck all day, listening and watching. Around two A.M. that night, hungry and thirsty, he set off for the formal garden. Miss Landry's offering lay in the ivy. He settled down upon it. Suddenly a beam of light shone on him, and Dr. Lockspur's voice shouted, "There! There!"

Tako ripped through the crab apple trees, took a long flying leap to the walk, another over the flowering quince hedge, and sprang to the park wall. He ran along it until he came to 109th Street. There he paused and glanced back. Men called and the hound bayed from the crab apples.

Tako waited for a taxi to pass, then he sprinted across the avenue and slipped into the storm sewer.

Dropping to the ledge, he crouched and waited.

It took the hound until daybreak to discover that Tako had taken to the wall for the bone meal reeked above the coyote odor. By this time the city was astir—cars moving, people starting to work.

Dr. Lockspur called off the dog. Cardy Evans snapped the leash on him.

Dr. Lockspur said, "Let's quit before we make the front page of the *Times*. You can't hunt coyotes by day in the City of New York. We'll have a howling crowd of animal lovers."

"We're close," said Cardy. "I'll wager he's on 109th Street."

However they did not pursue the hunt, but went to the Health Department car parked on the walk by the tool shed and drove off to rest.

As the morning brightened Tako dozed, listening nervously for a sound that was missing from the dawn. In his half-sleep he could not focus his mind on what it was, but there was a silence where there should have been a stir. He made a nest in the leaves and papers that were stuck in the storm sewer.

At dark a loud baying awakened him. The hound was barking at the grating, his nose so close that Tako could smell his breath. There was no way out but down. Tako slipped over the edge of the water catcher and dropped six feet. He hit the stone-lined tunnel, glanced up at the dog, and turned right.

"He can't be there!" Cardy said.

"He must be," Dr. Lockspur insisted. "Where's the light?"

A bus driver on his way home in the dusk paused and stared at the two men who were shining a light down the storm sewer. "New Yorkers will do anything, won't they?" he observed philosophically. He looked down the now grateless hole for the man he supposed the officials were after. "What's he doing down there?"

Two young girls from Barbados, seeking their fortunes as inspectors in the garment district of New York, saw the bus driver staring. They stopped, too. Laughing and talking in Spanish, they waited to see what was happening. They were joined by a woman taxi driver, then by a young Negro on his way to night classes at New York University. Others gathered. The hound bayed.

Dr. Lockspur was annoyed, but went on with his work. "We need a ladder," he said to Cardy. "I'm not going to jump down there."

Cardy Evans pointed to number 35 and asked the N. Y. U. student to borrow a ladder from the janitor. The young man hurried across the street and returned promptly with an aluminum one. The crowd pushed back while Cardy lowered the ladder.

"Wonder what TV network it is," the bus driver said to the student.

"Network? It's an advertising agency. There're no cameras."

"They always hide them," the woman taxi driver said.

The door of number 35 opened and Leon came out. He crossed the street slowly and stood beside the student. He watched Cardy Evans and Dr.

Lockspur disappear into the bowels of the city. Dr. Lockspur looked up, saw him, and called, "Can you hand me the dog, Leon?" His voice echoed and re-echoed. The lady taxi driver shrugged and hurried on to complete her business; the student looked at his watch and ran for the bus.

A window opened across the street. Tenny and her mother leaned out. Mrs. Harkness watched with interest, but Tenny bit her lip and turned away.

Tako heard the men descending.

The storm sewer was damp and dark. Sounds rumbled and echoed down the long stone tunnels. Water splashed and gushed. What Tako could not see he could hear, and the trickling of another sewer under Fifth Avenue lured him on. He paused at the junction. One pipe led straight to Central Park. His impulse was to take it. His intelligence, however, told him to confuse his hunters. He turned right, trotted a block north, then headed west. Not much water flowed from the park line, and he splashed in relative comfort for some distance.

Presently he came to a sparkle on the water. Glancing up he saw a street light shining through another opening. He leaped up to the high ledge, lay on his side, and shoved out through the narrow inlet. He was near the 110th Street boat house.

Tako glanced around and listened. The street sounded normal. The sewer, however, reverberated with hound bays. They were confused notes, for the dog could not follow the coyote's trail in the water. Tako cleaned his fur, then sped around Harlem Meer, over the Mount, and across paths and roads to the service building and the truck. He rolled in the bone meal, then crawled among the flats.

Just before dawn the tap of strange footsteps awoke him. A man was walking around the front of

the truck. He paced away, came back, and thumped himself down on the fender. His legs swung impatiently.

Mr. Hansen arrived. The man jumped to the ground.

"Are you a gardener?"

"Yes?"

"I'm from *The New York Times*. Har Lingal's the name. Pleased to meetcha."

Mr. Hansen mumbled a greeting.

"There's a rumor going around about a coyote in Central Park. Someone told me you might know something about him?"

"No sprechen Englischen," Mr. Hansen replied, and smiled blankly.

"Oh, for heaven's sake," said Mr. Lingal. "Come on. You do so."

"No sprechen Englischen," Mr. Hansen repeated, and smiled again.

"A coyote! Doggie. Wild doggie. Where is he?"

"No spreche. Me Danish." Mr. Hansen smiled once more and got into the cab.

That day he drove Tako to the bowling greens. While he worked the coyote slept securely. Mr. Hansen would chuckle now and then, pleased that the coyote was outwitting the men. Just before noon he paused on his rake and scanned the park, wondering why it was so filled with people on such a cold winter day.

Two days later Dr. Lockspur gave up searching the sewers. He had another plan. Early one morning he went to the formal garden and sat himself on the edge of the fountain. When Miss Landry arrived he stepped forward to meet her.

"Good morning," he said. Miss Landry pulled her coat tighter and turned her face away. "I'm sorry," he went on. He was well aware of her attitude. "I don't mean to offend you but I need some information from you."

"Oh?"

"It's more about the coyote."

"Oh, that. I read about that little episode in the paper. It's all over. The article said they trapped him in the sewer."

She opened her paper bag. The pigeons winged to the ground like a sudden rainstorm. Dr. Lockspur stepped back as one hovered over him, then alighted on his shoulder. He brushed it off nervously.

"These things carry infectious diseases," he mumbled before going back to his point. "We didn't get him. That story was premature. But it did put an end to thousands of inquiries about wild dogs and plagues. Also"—and he looked exasperated—"millions of suggestions as to how to catch him and billions of coyote helpers coming to feed him. The place has been overrun with people bringing hamburgers, apple pies, and even chocolate cake to the park. And that makes for a rat problem."

Miss Landry did not react. He went on.

"The article sort of quieted things down. With the pressure off I can work better. I notice you bring him meat every evening."

"Oh," she said quickly. "It's for the duck hawk, the peregrin falcon I feed. He lives in building tops as if they were river cliffs." She smiled.

"No, you don't feed him," he said. "A man reported him to the police. Said he was killing his racing pigeons. The falcon's been shot."

Miss Landry's face changed from properness to shock. "That's a sin!" she cried out. "That's immoral. That bird was the only thrilling thing left in New York City. It was very rare . . . and very wonderful."

"I know. I had nothing to do with it."

"Oh, oh, you people," she said and clenched her paper bag. Her voice shook with anger and sadness. "I don't think we need to talk any further.

The death of a beautiful falcon is too terrible to think about." She turned.

"Miss Landry," Dr. Lockspur said with exasperation, "the United States Government needs your cooperation. I would like to ask you to put down this piece of meat tonight. It has a cyanide pill in it."

"I will not! You do it!" She pushed past him.

"I've tried," he said. "He's smart. He knows my scent. He'll not come near anything I've touched. But with your odor on it, it would be different."

"I'll have nothing to do with it," she snapped. "It would kill me, not the coyote." Her back stiffened and her steps were determined as she walked toward the stairs to Fifth Avenue. She buried her sadness, for she knew that she could not bring the coyote any more meat. The men would certainly find it and figure out a way to poison it themselves.

Dr. Lockspur watched her go.

These crazy bird feeders, he said to himself. The animal is a threat, a danger, and no one will understand; no one cares. Well, I care. He wiped his forehead and walked to a phone booth to call Cardy Evans. As he passed the truck he banged his fist on the fender. The noise startled Tako. He awoke and sniffed. A low growl issued from his throat as he caught the scent of Dr. Lockspur.

The Chase

The days wore on. The circle tightened. Many live traps were set along the park trails, and the woods were filled with not one man with a hound, but six. No more beef chunks from Miss Landry were left in the ivy. Tako was disconcerted. The handout not only had been tasty, but had saved him time and given him an opportunity to concentrate on the hunt. But he was capable. He dug out a rat family near the garden, reaping, at last, the harvest near at hand, preserved by the coyote for emergencies.

Early one night when the dogs and men had left the park Tako slipped out of the truck for a drink. When he came back the truck was gone. A mechanic had taken it to the garage for repairs. Tako was homeless. He waited in the yew hedge until the sound of traffic lowered and the rats came out. Then he got up. He went over the wall and down 109th Street. He was hungry.

The scents of Dr. Lockspur and Cardy Evans were not around. At number 35 he checked the stairs. Tenny's scent was serene, calm. The sense of her well-being passed to him. Tako relaxed and glanced up at the buildings. He had a safe retreat —the roof tops. Above the city he knew there were niches and hideouts among chimneys and towers.

There was also food. He slipped down the street, crossing the avenues gingerly until he came to Rancid's block. Here he took the other side of the street to avoid a conflict that might bring on another onslaught of people.

When he came to the house of the pigeons he sprang to the fire escape and, tail low, moved silently to the roof. He was flying over the parapet when the warning came. The scent of Dr. Lockspur and Cardy Evans drenched the air.

The men had come to the pigeon owner's house after Dr. Lockspur had talked to Miss Landry. In thinking over the story of the falcon, the mammalogist had begun to wonder how the bird could open a cage. He decided to check.

Dr. Lockspur arranged to meet Herb after work. Herb joined him at five and together they climbed the stairs to the pigeon cage. Dr. Lockspur studied it, knowing full well no falcon had taken the birds. He said so.

"Then it *was* that cat," Herb replied. "Here's where he got in."

Dr. Lockspur examined the break. "It was no cat," he stated. "Not even Rancid is strong enough to tear this open. Besides—" and he leaned closer "—it looks as if canine teeth had torn it. A cat can't bite that way; he has to get an object back to his molars."

"The coyote?" Herb whispered in astonishment. "Then you mean he's real?"

"The coyote is real," Dr. Lockspur replied. He pulled a tuft of tawny fur from one of the broken wires. "The lab will verify this, but I'm ready to go ahead. If we wait long enough he will return."

"You gonna sit here and wait?"

"No," he replied thoughtfully. "We'll rig an electric eye . . ." He walked toward the fire escape. "On the front of the building. The coyote comes over this way because there's no other way up . . . and we'll attach it to a buzzer."

He paused as he looked down upon the city. "I saw a 'room for rent' sign on your door. I'll check out of the hotel and stay here . . . and we'll have to use a rifle."

"Rifle?"

"He's trap smart. That means he knows what they are and how to spring them. And now he's hound wary—holes up somewhere by day and sneaks out at night. We've pressured him a little too much in the park. He'll come here. He's still bound by routine. He's still an animal."

"Pretty clever though, eh?" said Herb softly.

"Yes, and I hate to say this but I'm beginning to like him too. May I use your phone to get Evans and an electrician?"

The electric trap was completed by sundown. After it was checked out, Cardy lingered in Dr. Lockspur's new room to discuss some other city health threats. Both men were draped in old Morris chairs when the buzzer went off. They stared at each other, then leaped.

Tako heard feet pummeling the stairs to the roof as he veered and leaped over the wall to the next building. He dropped low, followed the shadows to the next house, and soared lightly to it.

A muffled shot rang out. Tako barely heard it, but instantly his left flank burned with pain. He tumbled head down onto the tarred roof, slid on his jaw, then got up. His left leg would not respond. The men were coming toward him. Pulling his leg against his body, he took off in a three-legged sprint.

"He can't get any further than Third Avenue," Dr. Lockspur shouted to Cardy as they climbed ungracefully over a parapet.

Tako passed a clothes basket and a water tower. He judged them and ran on. He had been a tricky hunter, now he could be a tricky prey. At the last

building he leaped onto the parapet and paused against the skyline to be in clear view of the men. They shouted and pointed. Tako then dropped into the shadows and came straight back toward them. Eyes and minds still on the silhouette on the Third Avenue horizon, they looked high. He passed low, leaped into a T-shaped chimney pot, and lay still. His leg throbbed.

Tako licked the wound to stop the flow of blood as he listened to the hunters. When their footsteps sounded at the correct distance, he jumped to the roof and ran west. They kept running east. Tako took the next fire escape down to the street.

He left the men looking behind boxes, around chimneys, and back of water towers, and slipped under a car to press himself painfully toward the park.

His leg was stiffening as he reached number 35 and crawled beneath the last automobile on the block, José's "Patchwork." Panting, he stared at the park. Then he tensed. The Street Family had ended a rehearsal on their steel drums, and were now milling out of number 35.

"It's late," José said to Elaine. "We'd better get some sleep or we'll drag tomorrow."

"I'm hungry," said Tenny. "Let's go to the Turk's for some ice cream."

"I can't," Maria said. "Mama wants me." She started home. Elaine joined her.

"I'd like a cone," José said. "Come on, Tenny, I'll treat. Give you some strength for tomorrow."

José and Tenny called good night to the rest of the Family and turned toward 110th Street.

Tako sensed he should bolt; but his leg bothered him and he had no plan. The men were not following him and the Street Family had vanished. He put his head down to rest.

A few minutes later Tenny and José returned, talked animatedly. They paused at the car. Tenny opened the door and sat on the seat to finish her cone.

"I hope I don't get nervous tomorrow at the audition," she said softly.

Her warm voice once more felt comforting to the coyote. Tako moved toward her. She lowered her hand, and there above him was cold, sweet ice cream. He reached up and took it. Tenny jumped. He pulled back.

"Tako!" she whispered and got down on her knees to look under the car. "Tako!" She stood up. "José, it's the coyote! He's alive! He's right here. What'll we do?"

Before José could answer Tenny had snatched his cone and was climbing into the back seat. She opened the door and held the ice cream below the car.

Tako came forward, lured by the cool sugariness, but more by Tenny's attitude. It awoke an old imprint . . . the sense of survival . . . like the first time he had met her. He licked the ice cream. She pulled back. He followed her into the car. She smiled and gently closed the door.

"You'll be all right for a little while," she whispered, and her hand came toward him. Then she saw the clot of blood on his leg. "He's wounded," she said in anguish. "They must have shot him. How awful."

José peered intently down the street. Suddenly he swung around the front of the car, sprang into the driver's seat, and started the engine.

"José," Tenny gasped. "What're you doing?"

"I don't know. Here come Cardy and that Albany man. Close the door." Tenny crawled over to the front seat and did as he said. The car moved out from the curb.

José turned down Fifth Avenue. "Tell me about coyotes. Where do they live?"

"I don't know, I don't know. Dr. Lockspur said some were in the Adirondacks." She twisted around in the seat. Then her voice dropped. "I got him into the city. I guess I'll have to get him out. But how?"

José pressed his foot on the accelerator. He turned into Central Park but did not stop. He drove out the other entrance.

"What are you doing, José?" Tenny cried.

"We're going to the Adirondacks."

"The Adirondacks?"

"Yes. I can't bear to turn him over to the cops for doing nothing but living. Someone did that to me once."

"But José—" Tenny slumped in the seat. Her voice came softly. "It's a long way. We won't be back in time for the audition."

"There'll be others."

Tenny's eyes misted. "It means a great deal to you . . . a job . . . José. Getting away from 109th Street and all the poverty . . ."

"Do you want to turn him in? He can't live around here if he's injured. It looks like a flesh wound. That's not so bad. He can hole up in the woods and make out."

Tenny leaned over the seat and spoke to Tako. Her voice was soft and reassuring.

As the car turned onto the northbound highway she put her head in her hands. "José," she whispered. "So much has happened to me since the day I walked into the city with a coyote. So much I can't tell you."

"Like what?" he asked.

"Mainly my crazy daydreams have disappeared," she answered. "I don't pretend I'm saving kids from fire or discovering a bomb in the mayor's office any more. You know why?"

He didn't answer.

"I've got friends." The corners of her lips curled softly. "And I've discovered that friends don't care

if you're not a saint. . . . I used to think they did.
I tried to be one; but I couldn't be, so I dreamed I
was."

"Then . . ." She leaned against the window and
looked out at the swishing horizon. "Then . . . I
let a coyote go. It was that simple. I just did an old
plain, thoughtless, well-meant, dumb act and everything began to change. . . . People gathered
around me, nice ones, angry ones, concerned ones.
But they were there—and it was nice. They hammered me into a 'people.'"

"Tenny, you are such a naive mothersistersweet-
heartoldmaid. Any gal who sets a coyote free in
New York City knowingly or unknowingly is no
saint. She is a lovable cloud watcher who steps on a
banana peel, plunks ungraciously and painfully on
her behind, and makes everyone laugh and cry."

"Who laughed?" she shouted hysterically. "It
wasn't funny."

José took a deep breath. "Oh, Tenny," he said in
exasperation, "you're so darned serious. . . . Let
me think . . . I know . . . The coyotes, honey,
the coyotes laughed and laughed . . . and, *petita*,
if you go out West today you will still hear them
laughing from hill to hill."

A giggle started in Tenny's chest. It became a

snicker, then a tinkling snuff, and, finally, a glorious laugh. Tears helped the laughter flow.

These sounds fell over Tako. He spread his paws in an instinctive reaction, as he had in the protective warmth near his coyote mother. All would be well.

The car sped on.

ABOUT THE AUTHOR

The enthusiastic reception that young people accord each new book by Jean George is warmly seconded by their parents, teachers, and librarians. Mrs. George is co-author of *Dipper of Copper Creek*, which received the Aurianne Award for the most outstanding animal story published in 1957. *My Side of the Mountain, The Summer of the Falcon, Gull Number 737*, and *Spring Comes to the Ocean* all have affirmed her remarkable sensitivity both to the world of nature and to young people.

Mrs. George is a regular contributor of nature stories to *Reader's Digest*. She has held the position of art editor for *Pageant* magazine and has served as a newspaper reporter for the *Washington Post* and International News Service.

ABOUT THE ARTIST

John Kaufmann was born in New York City and attended the Art Students League, as well as the Pennsylvania Academy of Fine Arts. He also studied at the Istituto Statale D'Arte in Florence, Italy. He has illustrated many children's books on subjects in the natural sciences, including Jean George's *The Moon of the Salamanders*. Watching birds in the New York area is a favorite hobby of his; as yet he has spotted no coyotes there!